Collages

Collages

21 Stories
from the
Complete Creative Writing Course

Edited by
Maggie Hamand
Natasha Hodgson
Emmanuelle Chazarin

CCWC

First published in 2013 by

The Complete Creative Writing Course
82 Forest Road, London E8 3BH
www.writingcourses.org.uk

A catalogue record of this book is available from the
British Library

ISBN 978-0-9576944-0-8

Designed by Jane Havell Associates

Printed and bound in the UK

Front cover photographs: Aden – Public Corporation for
Tourism, Ari Bakker, Sara Biljana, Jimmy Brown, Bárbara
Cannela, Emmanuelle Chazarin, Eljay, Frank Hamand,
Maggie Hamand, Emilio Labrador, Kyle May, Gregory
Moine, Patel, Bill Strain, Gill Vaux, Zyllan Fotografía

Contents

Foreword

THIS IS THE SECOND ANTHOLOGY of writing from the Complete Creative Writing Course. All the writers have attended at least one of our courses and some have been with us for several terms. Each story has developed from a sketchy start, and through a process of feedback, discussion and constructive criticism in class, followed by a professional editing process, has developed into a striking and original piece of work.

The stories are remarkably diverse in theme, setting and style and reflect the huge variety of voices in contemporary London. Historical, contemporary and futuristic, dealing with intimate human relationships or big themes, each has a unique appeal and, taken together as a collection, they should challenge and delight a wide audience.

We would like to thank our editors and readers Natalie Butlin, Emmanuelle Chazarin and Natasha Hodgson; Jane Havell for design and typesetting; Emmanuelle Chazarin and Jane Havell for the cover design, and the team of tutors at CCWC: Karen Falconer, Catherine Johnson, Kolton Lee and Naomi Wood.

ARIKE OKE

Last Days in Loware

THE MORNINGS HERE are airless. The heat presses down: a layer of hot sand trickling over me until I'm covered. Every night I moisturise my hands and face. Every morning I wake up with chapped lips and skin on the turn to flaking. I keep water in a bottle by my bed. I drink it, imagining a swimming pool filling slowly, dry leaves and twigs of dreams rising and spinning and floating.

I can't bear for Rupe to touch me in the night; the heat is everywhere between us and on us. He leaves in the morning with considerate discretion. In England the depression his body left in the bed was a cool valley, a tangible absence. This bed is hard and it retains no impression of him.

Seeing Rupe at dinner sometimes feels like meeting a ghost, or a memory. I'm light-headed, and he is preoccupied. He lets the fingers of his left hand float up and touch his ear in a constant return. I want to chew on him to convince myself he's really here. Rupe doesn't tolerate that kind of behaviour, of course. I take hold of both of his hands and kiss him on his eyelids, which always flutter shut as I come near. He pulls slightly away.

'It's just so hot,' I try to explain, 'at night. And then when I wake up you're not there.' I begin to say, 'It's like being in hell,' but stop myself in time. 'It's like being in a furnace,' I say instead, thinking of the sort that cremates bodies.

Rupe says, 'You could turn the air conditioning on,' and gives me a glancing kiss on the cheek as he turns away to unwrap his tie.

'I can't,' I say, 'you know it gives me earache.'

*

In the daytime, while Rupe is at the High Commission, I get the driver to take me around the city. Here in Loware my driver is Joseph. Joseph is not interested in talking with me, but the car does have air conditioning. The muffled sort, not the harassing type we have in our bedroom. I feel poised in the car's cool climate, like a cucumber waiting to be selected from a supermarket chiller cabinet. The car moves through Loware, murmuring to itself. Outside, the traffic clamours.

Joseph's choice to be mute is abnormal, in my experience. Usually people are pretty anxious to make me understand what their country is all about.

As they see it.

When we lived in Tonga, Epony arranged for me to visit dancers in rehearsal. The male dancers clapped, and made sudden shouts, while the women slowly gestured, singing. I felt naked, watching them perform traditional movement while I looked on, not understanding. Epony petted me afterwards. She stroked my arm as I looked out of the window of the residence there. I stared into the greens of the garden. There were hundreds of shades of green. I could still hear drums beating in my ears. 'You see,' Epony told me, 'much history here. It's as I said.'

Joseph remains aloof, however, when I try to engage him in conversation. I want to visit the market; there must be one. I imagine the colours and the women shoving past one another to squeeze fruit. I imagine the rancid smell of trodden vegetables. I imagine a hubbub.

I ask Joseph, 'Where's the best place to buy mangoes?'

He tells me, 'Madam, the cook has already bought mangoes.'

'Thank you, Joseph,' I say, 'but I think Mrs Delonge has plans for those mangoes already, and I would like to visit a typical market. Maybe I will make a fruit salad for my husband,' I say, appealing to his machismo. I add, 'Do you know of anywhere that sells limes?'

I catch a glimpse of Joseph's unguarded attention in the rear-view mirror. I almost have him. But then he flickers back into staring in a fixed line down the centre of the carriageway. Mustard earth and white-boned bushes frame the road as we leave the zone where the residence is. The residence is one among many exhausted white-washed buildings, each encased in their own fortress compounds. Joseph doesn't know why I bother leaving the compound. I can tell by the way he sucks in his cheek when I ask him to bring the car around. The sun shears across the razor bumps which dot his face. I am interrupting his routine. He cleans the car twice a day. It gleams for a few hours and then the dust settles in a yellow patina.

Away from the residential district, buildings leer. They bleed rust-coloured streaks down their sides. They have painted tin signs. They wheeze in the heat, with no compound wall to buffer them from the streets. People mill in and out of the buildings. So many of them wear the stiff African textiles. They look like orchid flowers, dried and blown about in a harmattan wind. The exceptions are the road users: the bus drivers, traffic policemen, boys riding bicycles improbably loaded up with things wrapped in plastic sheeting and rope. These people all yell at one another. I open the window a crack and sound comes in, rolling into the car in a tidal wave: engines coughing, voices raised in greetings and arguments, static and tinny pop music. I look at faces that pass us in their vehicles and see teeth gleam as songs come crashing out of their radios.

'Madam, it's not good,' Joseph says.

I wind the window back up.

Dusty rusting cars, minibuses and bicycles travel past us in the opposite direction; ours is the only car slugging obstinately away on Joseph's mystery route. 'Perhaps they know something we don't,' I say to him.

Without turning he shrugs his shoulders and says, 'It's market day.'

I don't know whether to laugh or not, so I cough, holding the noise against my lips with the corner of my sleeve. Outside the car, dirt thrown up from the road swirls in the air. Particles of mica twinkle in the sunlight as though caught in an equatorial snow globe.

Joseph swerves to avoid something in the road. I look out of my window at the thing. It looks like a body. I'm sure it's a body – I see fingers curling at the end of an arm outstretched. Joseph keeps driving. I watch road dust settle over the body. 'Joseph.' I try to draw his attention.

Joseph's head is a silhouette around which the sun licks. His voice tick-tocks with no emotion, 'Madam, someone will take care of it.'

*

This evening we're hosting a dinner at our residence, in keeping with the low-key, semi-informal approach Rupe has been told to take here. It's my first opportunity to host in Loware, but I'm not worried; my guests have always commented on how I manage to hit just the right tone. Rupe says this quality I have, of making everyone feel welcome, is why he married me. I have Mrs Delonge prepare dishes that represent the local cuisine, and that include mangoes. I arrange for chrome buckets to be filled with ice and for blue and green glass bottles of water to go into these buckets, as well as prominently placed bottles of champagne. I've booked wine waiters. The glasses are filled with champagne in the kitchen, but I know that it makes an impression to have chilled bottles on show as well. At least, to me it does: look at how much ice I have. We're holding the dinner in the Cavendish Hall, a big long room that still retains a colonial-era elegance. Instead of air conditioning this room has ceiling fans. They stir the brothy air.

Rupe's PA Naomi sent me briefing notes on the guests last week. Rupe, for once, wanted to go through the list with me.

'You don't have to speak with all of them,' he said. I could see blue veins through the thin skin under his eyes. 'Some of these characters are pretty unsavoury. Just keep circulating. Keep the mood light. Don't get into deep discussions.'

'No deep discussions,' I said, and gave him my little finger to hook with his. 'I promise.'

*

The unofficial theme for tonight is 'cultural exchange'. The subtext is we're to give the military government a chance to be pictured off duty. 'We're all friends here' – that sort of thing. I'm excited about the artists on the guest list, but not so much the generals. Rupe tells me not to expect the artists to stay long. There is only one local writer on the guest list, but he has declined the invitation. The other intelligentsia attending are in Loware at the university, or are in the country on sponsored projects. Loware once had an ancient library, back in the age of the Malian Empire. It's gone now, but there are traces of archaeology. They draw people here.

I remembered Epony's Tongan lesson and asked Naomi to put me in touch with a well-reviewed jali performer. A kind of bard, Kouleko, arrived early and indulged me by teaching me some melodies on his kora. He showed me how to nestle the girth of the hollowed-out calabash in my lap. It smelt of markets, with a rubbed mustiness rising from the stretched cow skin. I plucked at the strings in the order Kouleko showed me, but the notes fell short in disappointed tuts. He laughed and said, 'You have to make friends with the kora before you pluck her.'

This evening, Kouleko plays a restrained set, and doesn't sing. There is a smattering of European faces here, and you can tell those Africans who grew up in Europe. They have a more pronounced edge to their civility, as if they're making a point. Whether it's for our benefit or their countrymen's it's hard to decide. The intellectuals stand apart from one another, and don't mix with the government men. It's actually a hard skill to avoid eye contact and remain polite, but my guests this evening are proficient at it.

I flit from person to person, making introductions, asking, 'Have you tried the mangoes yet?'

The Afro-Europeans thank me stiffly for the hospitality. Iwedu, the acclaimed poet, is clearly making the most of the champagne. He is effusive: he tells me, 'Beautiful, delightful,' using vowels that hang precariously between consonants. Occasionally I look around for Rupe. He's usually nodding and listening with professional focus. I spot him in a corner with General Esango. The general uses a white handkerchief to dab at his face. It doesn't seem to be helping. I see damp patterns forming where his collar holds stiff against his neck.

'You're working hard,' says a little, young, white man I come across in my third circuit of the room.

'Oh, no, an evening like this is just lovely, such fun,' I counter, running through lists of names in my mind. I cross through those I've already spoken to, so he is not Amon, the freelance correspondent for some UK broadsheets. He's possibly late twenties, I calculate, appraising the length of time he'll let his fringe fall into his eyes before he shakes it out. English-sounding. 'You're the artist – Titch Ellis – I loved the work you made for the Wayfarer Festival last April.'

Titch quivers a little. His mousy fine hair falls into his eyes. He blinks and uses the heel of a hand to push his hair back out of his face. 'Impressive,' he says. 'Can you do that for everyone here?'

'Who do you want to know about?'

Titch allows his eyes to drop down me. His eyes track across my painted toes, barely visible; the layers of silk spun with cotton and dyed a calming lavender that make up my dress ; my cheeks, lightly reddened with drink and hospitality; the strands of hair that stick to my neck with the sweat that, despite the ceiling fans, still prickles me. I haven't been this looked-at for a long time.

Titch's eyes lazily find mine. I stare back at him; I don't think I need to be polite to everyone after all.

'What sort of art are you doing here?' I ask, and take a fluted glass from one of the waiters.

'I'm recording sounds,' Titch says. It's a voice he uses for people from whom he doesn't expect comprehension. Other people use that voice on me. 'It's, well, I'm interested in authenticity. It's all about authenticity.'

'Are you recording sounds tonight?' I ask.

Titch's mouth twitches at the corner. It's a small mouth. It looks like it wants to be a wide, expressive mouth, but must make do with what it has.

'I'd think some of the people in this room would relish any chance to go down in history,' I say.

'They're cardboard,' Titch says. 'History's moving them around. I'm talking real people – the people who are affected by the whim of these nonsense figures in here. The people whose lives go on, go on loving, go on arguing, go on eating and crying and bartering, even when the paper autocracies these idiots make disintegrate around them.'

'Bartering? Have you been to the market? I'd love to see it, what's it like?'

Titch says, 'Excuse me, my funder's over there.' He walks off towards a woman, older than me; her glasses are rimless and her hair is styled into stiff blonde waves curling high over a tall forehead. Lady Chester, my memory gives me the name, the trustee of the Commonwealth Council. I see her mouth open wide with the word, 'Titch,' and I see Titch enthusiastically kiss her cheek and shake the hand of General Sanyo, who is standing with Lady Chester.

General Sanyo has always impressed me with his repulsion of the heat; I've never seen him sweat, despite wearing a thick cotton army uniform. It's hard to imagine him, a man with deep dimples and an impressive ability to seem at ease with everyone, giving orders for a woman journalist to be kicked to death. That's what Rupe told me off the record about him. Even Rupe can be shocked into indiscretion. Titch looks back at me and starts when he finds me still watching him. He nods at me and turns back to Lady Chester and the general.

*

It's a tiring evening, after all. I'm glad when it's time to go to bed, until I remember the heat in our room. Rupe says he still has some work to finish. He sits in his office, his face illuminated by his laptop. I watch him from the doorway for a while. The blue light makes shadows sit in the furrows of his face.

'Is everything all right?' I ask him.

He squints up at me. It takes his eyes a moment to adjust to the light from the doorway. 'Everything that we have any power over is fine,' he says. 'Go to bed.'

'Can I open the windows?' I ask.

'No, darling,' Rupe says, his eyes are back on the computer. 'There are too many mosquitoes.'

*

Months later, after we have been evacuated and relocated to a residence in a country full of lakes, Rupe's PA calls me.

'Sorry to disturb,' Naomi says. 'It's been tied up. For a while.' She speaks like that, with so much efficiency you have to run along to pick up the thread. 'It's all cleared now, so, if you're okay to receive it I'll send it along. Titch Ellis. Email. Okay?'

I allow a pause, so that it seems that I am trying to place Titch's name. 'Yes, fine, please do forward it. No problem. Thanks.' I mimic her bullet-point phrasing.

She's too busy to notice. 'Great. It's burned to CD now, of course. Will send over.'

*

When the CD arrives a day later, I take it into Rupe's study and close all the windows. I think about closing the curtains as well, but I leave them as they are. I get a glass of ice water and sit in Rupe's armchair, with my journal on my knee. In the envelope with the CD is a print-out of an email. It doesn't look like much has been redacted, but how could I tell? It reads: 'Market sounds for you. Authentic. Recorded 11th February 2011. Titch.'

The CD is only five minutes long. Titch doesn't speak on it. I hear shuffling feet, horns, duelling shouts, crackling plastic, poultry noises, chopping sounds, barking, cats or babies crying. These sounds tally with my imagined Loware market. I remember the heat again. My body sinks into the chair. I close my eyes to imagine the women to whom those shuffling feet belong. Are they wearing flip-flops? The smell of the market hits me. I think it smells of burning rubber, and also of sweaty armpits and soured condensed milk. I listen harder. Is that Titch breathing? I open my journal and take out the newspaper clippings folded inside. The top one is clipped from *The Telegraph*. It has yellowed already. I should have kept it away from sunlight.

Titch Ellis, hailed as a leading figure in the 'approaching storm' of the next generation of young British artists, which include Ariadne Marshall and Lu Liden in their number, is missing pre-sumed dead after riots in the eponymous capital city of Loware, West Africa.

Ellis was based in Loware working on a new commission, the content of which was a closely guarded secret. Even Ellis's patrons, the Commonwealth Council, were not privy to the full details of his latest project. 'We were expecting something out of the ordinary from Titch Ellis,' said spokesperson Anna Millton, 'We gave him free reign within a skeleton brief of "Middle Earth: Within the Equator". Loware was the first of what were to be a series of residences across West and Central Africa.'

Ellis came to prominence when his solo exhibition 'Ten and a Half Years' in Tunnels, the emerging artist space in Edin-burgh, divided critical opinion and led to a controversial ban on the use of amplification equipment in the disused underground chambers of the local university. What Ellis would have produced from this latest project may never be known, but he had done enough to assure his place in the national art consciousness, at least for the current generation.

None of the clippings I've collected contain details on what might have happened to the recordings he made. Parts of his body were recovered from the market after the riots were put down but no recording equipment was reported found with him. His apartment had been gutted. Nothing of him remained in Loware except for macheted pieces of body and clothing, eventually repatriated. And now, in my hands, this CD. The email is dated just eight days before the first riot, sent to Rupe's office. I wonder why I didn't receive it then.

I'm still sitting in Rupe's chair, in his study, with all the windows closed, when he returns from the embassy. I can hear him searching through the residence for me. Eventually I call out to him as he passes the study door.

'What are you doing in here?' he asks. His voice is gentle – 'With all the windows shut on a warm day like this?'

ANGELA YOUNG

For the Love of Life

1

I AM STANDING in the corner of a small hospital room. My charge, a girl born less than an hour ago, lies lifeless across her mother's stomach. The length of the mother's white hand spans the child's tiny body. A starched sheet covered with speckles and splotches of blood is pulled up over the mother's hips. The mother's face is turned towards me, her eyes red-rimmed, her mouth pulled open in a silent howl, but she can't see me.

I stretch out my arms. I mean to relieve her of the cause of her sorrow. I mean to show her my arms are the only safe place for her child, now. But she lifts the little girl, gently, carefully, and holds her against her heart. And then she sends a shout of fury in my direction and my arms fall, shaking, to my sides. So loud is the mother's shout that I wonder if she *can* see me, even though I know the only people who can see us here, in your world, are those we've come to collect.

A single candle burns on the other side of the bed. I narrow my eyelids until the candle flame is all I can see. I am used to anger and I am used to sorrow; we all are. And, because of the war, we are more than usually prepared. I focus on the candle flame and wait. The wail of an air-raid siren insinuates itself into the room and then Matron walks in. She pulls the blackout curtains across the window and then she pulls down the anti-splinter blind. She takes hold of the white rail at the foot of the bed and begins to move the bed towards the door. But the mother shouts and swears: she tells Matron to leave them where they are.

The candle flame flickers.

Matron says, 'That language will not do, Mrs Wells. It will not do at all. There are other mothers and babies to consider.'

'If you leave us alone,' says the mother, 'they won't hear me.'

'Patients must be moved to the corridors during an air raid,' says Matron. 'By order of the Ministry of Home Security.'

Some truly foul words fly from the mother's mouth and matron straightens up, smoothes down her uniform and leaves the bed at an awkward angle across the room. 'On your own head be it,' she says, as she leaves.

I stand stock still in my corner. I can feel the thick felt of the anti-splinter blind behind my shoulder. I shift away from it just as the planes begin their grinding hum above us. And then the bombs begin to fall. They whistle, they growl, they crump and they destroy. It is alarming, even to me, but the mother is unmoved. She lies on her bed with her child across her heart. She devotes her entire attention to her child; she talks to her as if she were merely asleep. And then another noise, a human noise, makes itself known under the sounds of the bombs. I look up. The child's mouth is open.

She is making a hoarse sound, like someone trying to breathe, or someone breathing their last. By the time the planes grind away from us and the raid is over (the hospital has been spared) the little girl's chest has begun to rise and fall falteringly, like a small bird's, and one of her arms makes a quick shuddering movement.

Although we are schooled to feel as little as possible when we arrive to collect our charges, I am astonished. Almost moved.

A shout of joy erupts from the mother's throat. She takes her daughter's little hand in hers and kisses it. She stands and struggles towards the door. She opens it and shouts for a doctor, but when he arrives he says, 'It's a reflex action, Mrs Wells.' He looks at her and holds out his hands. 'You must allow us to take her now.'

He speaks gently but he is met with a monumental roar.

'You may not take her! Not while she lives!'

Her hand shakes as it reaches behind her for the bed.

'I must insist,' says the doctor, but his voice is weak and he doesn't make any attempt to take my charge from her mother's arms, and then all is eerily quiet.

The doctor whispers into the silence, 'I will send Matron.' But it sounds as if he is saying, 'I will send reinforcements.' He backs out of the small hospital room, his stethoscope swinging as he fumbles for the door handle.

I am as winded as he.

The mother, holding her daughter tightly to her, lies back on her bed. She pulls the speckled, splotched sheet over them both. I close my eyes and, as the darkness gathers behind my eyelids, a joyous sound fills the room. The mother is singing *Bye, Baby Bunting* to her child.

A surprising smell of coffee seeps in through the ventilation brick behind me. And then the smell of cordite that always comes with the bombs seeps in too. When I open my eyes I see a weak red light through the lattice and I realise the fires have started. I am not facing the bed but I know I am being watched and when I can no longer resist the force that wants me to look at it (I have resisted because I'm afraid of it) I turn back and see a pair of brilliant blue eyes staring straight into mine.

They dazzle me, those eyes. They make me tremble. They set my heart beating quickly. There is defiance in their expression, but no horror. And behind the defiance there is infinite tenderness. This has never happened to me before and I don't know what to do. I look away but the sheer force of the child's presence makes me look back. And then she shows me what to do.

She widens her eyes and her bright blue gaze pierces my heart until I feel as if I have been burned, from the inside. And then, magisterially slowly, she closes her eyelids and I am reduced to tears. She has dismissed me.

*

'It's as if I've been hypnotised. I keep seeing her eyes. I can't get them out of my head. I've never seen such beauty . . . they were . . . I felt . . .'

'They were alive,' says Sariel.

'I know. But . . .'

'I don't think you've quite grasped what's happened to you.'

'I haven't had the heart to volunteer for another charge.'

'It's too *much* heart you're suffering from,' says Sariel.

I stare at him. Sometimes he gets there before we do. But then that's his job. He's the boss.

I look away from him and realise I've put my hand on my heart. I keep doing it. Ever since I came back without my last charge, ever since she burned me, branded me, I've had this feeling I can't remember having before. At least not since I've been a messenger. It's an aching fizzing feeling, as if my heart's expanding, as if it's exploding, but gently, beautifully, like a flower opening and opening and opening.

'When life chooses to touch you, you have to make a choice,' says Sariel.

I shake my head and he stares at me as if I'm some kind of idiot.

'You got a first,' he says. 'You were one of my best students. You can't have forgotten *everything*.'

'It's different when it happens,' I say. 'When it's real. These feelings are so . . . overwhelming.' I stare at him, helplessly. I shrug. He smiles.

'Yes,' says Sariel, 'they are.' And then he turns away, bent over, as if he is in pain. I'm surprised to feel a prickling behind my eyes and my heart contracts in sympathy. I'm not used to such feelings. We are taught to shut down our feelings, we have to when we collect our charges, otherwise we'd make mistakes. So it's a habit here, with every-one.

'It's painful to remember,' says Sariel. 'You are reminding me.'

I've never seen the boss uncertain before and I don't know what to do. I stretch out my hand, tentatively, and he turns quickly, before I can pretend I meant to do something other than touch him. He takes my hand and I gasp. We never touch each other because we must not get into the habit: we must only touch our charges when our hands can no longer do any harm.

'You must choose, Gregory,' says Sariel, again. He hardly ever calls us by our given names. 'And however you choose, your work will change, forever. But if you choose to stay with her, in her world, on earth . . .' His voice tails off.

'Has it happened to you?' I say, realising as I ask that of course it has.

'Yes,' he says and I get the distinct feeling he doesn't want to say any more, but I must know. How can I decide if I don't know?

'And?'

'It is a gift beyond anything, if you can find the strength for it.'

He takes a deep breath and looks at me through tear-filled eyes, a sight I've never seen before.

'It is the most wonderful, uplifting, extraordinary, some would say God-given experience. But in return for this rarest of gifts, you must make a sacrifice.' He squeezes my hand and lets it go.

'Did you?'

He turns away and then he turns back and looks straight at me.

'Of course I did,' says Sariel. 'Of course I did.'

2

I chose to return.

I had no more idea than you how it would be, but it didn't require much courage: the pull of those brilliant blue eyes was impossible to resist. The thought of them eclipsed everything. I didn't think about the consequences, the way people don't when they fall in love.

Fools rush in . . .

Sariel said I could ask him for help any time from now until . . . well, until it ends. But he also said coming back would be more difficult each time. He said he thought I wouldn't manage to ask his advice more than thrice. He never uses words like thrice.

He gave me a scarlet handkerchief. He said I should tie a knot in it each time I made a mistake or didn't know what to do next. He said I should meditate on the knot. He said the answers were inside me and the handkerchief was a focus, a locus, for what I already embodied. All I had to do was find it. He said the chief difference between what I was about to do and being an ordinary messenger was that I couldn't *do* anything. I must watch and wait for longer than I would believe possible and, eventually, the right time would come. She would show me. He said I must remind myself of that when things got difficult. And then he wished me luck and I left, and I have been watching Sarah ever since.

She is so very alive. She kicks and she calls; she smiles and she gurgles; she pulls herself up and stands in her cot; she stares with absolute attention when the wind moves the faded yellow curtain, when the shadows fall, when the lamp lights the cracks that criss-cross the ceiling, when sunlight makes a shaft on the wall.

She was about eighteen months old when she learned to climb over the rail of her cot. Sometimes she lost her balance and fell. At least twice she fell at an awkward angle and I longed to pick her up and soothe her, make sure she wasn't hurt, do whatever was necessary, but of course I couldn't. I must never touch her. But her lungs are strong and she can summon her mother with ease and she, being a nurse, always knows what to do.

I have watched Sarah by the river that runs beneath the mill opposite their cottage. The mill race is quick but although I can see she would like to touch it, the way it wrenches sticks from her hands frightens her. The part of the river she loves, where it slows and bends in on itself, like an arm bent at the elbow, is where I have watched her the most. She squats on the bank for hours. She watches the ducks and the swans with their young; she talks to them and they seem to listen to her. She stares into the water as if it will provide her with answers to her questions. She talks to herself about what she can see: the fish; the flowing weed; the stones; the ripples; the glints and sparkles; the birds; the colours; the shallows; the deeps. She throws leaves or sticks into the water and watches them float away. She frowned when first she saw a water vole paddling to the opposite bank and then the loveliest smile lit up her little face as she bent and turned in her attempts to see its burrow.

'A swimming mouse,' she said to herself. 'It's a swimming mouse.'

Even when she is still she is not idle. She seems to ripple just as the river ripples. When a heron stands on one leg she copies him. When a swan rises from the water she makes wings with her arms and runs along the riverbank. When the postman arrives on his bicycle she holds out her hands, hopping from foot to foot.

I could watch her forever.

I shall watch her forever.

Once I thought she saw me and my heart leapt. It was winter. Slabs of ice sheathed the cold water beneath the snow-covered banks. A sudden desire to touch the ice filled me. Before I could reason with myself, before I could stop myself, I knelt down and stretched out my hand. But when my fingers touched the ice it cracked and split and Sarah, who was making a snowman on the opposite bank, turned quickly to look. In her speed she lost her footing and slid towards the freezing river. One foot hooked itself round the bole of a young aspen and she dug the other deep into the snow, grasped the tree with her small hands and then, it seemed in slow motion, she turned and stared straight at me, her blue eyes filled with that same brilliance, that same dazzling defiance I had seen in the hospital.

I was pathetically grateful that she had, at last, noticed me. But she shrank from me, a horrified expression on her sweet face. She turned and ran up the riverbank, between the alders, over the low wall and across the lane to her cottage. As I watched her leave me, I cried. My throat ached. I thought of Sariel as the tears flowed down my cheeks in warm rivulets and I understood, for the first time, what he meant. For what Sarah's eyes told me, in the only glance she had given me in seven long years, was that I was an ugly thing. I, who loved her young soul with all my heart, was repellent to her.

Why had I ever thought it could be otherwise?

I pulled the red handkerchief from my pocket and, with shaking hands, tied the first knot.

BELINDA SADDINGTON

An African Death

1

DAMP WITH DESIRE is no way to arrive at a meeting with the headmaster. I close the door to the flat behind me but leave my coat open so the cold February air will cool me down. Earl's Court Road is busy even at this early hour and I weave through people like a rugby player, though this is no open green playing field; it's a narrow cracked pavement lit by street lamps, shop windows and a stream of passing cars. The school is only a short distance away but I am late. I should have said, 'No, sorry, I don't do meetings before nine a.m.' But instead I agreed to it. And now I am hurrying to meet him when I could have stayed home in bed with her, with Lara. I hate the headmaster.

I break into a slow jog, which is a little lopsided because of the bloody great briefcase in my right hand. I come to the Cromwell Road and stop. Moving car lights come from every direction and I can't quite make out when the cars have actually stopped. The red man on the traffic light opposite me is a ludicrously long way away. When he goes green, I walk across very quickly and turn right along the pavement bordering the dual carriageway. I refuse to go any faster. An image of Lara comes to me: the way she was, curvy and warm, just about half an hour ago, in my bed, when I could have run the tip of my index finger along the soft, smooth skin of her bare shoulder and hooked the sheet further down to uncover her completely. I'm starting to boil. Focus, man. Where is that blasted little side road that leads to the school? I've walked past it several times over the years. It's there, next left, 'Wolverton Way', and it's like entering another world; eerily quiet despite its proximity to a main road.

Steven Duggan, headmaster of the London School of Nations, will guess where I've been, of course. And from experience, I think he'll seem jovial at first, his big body at ease, half-smile on his generous lips. But then he'll stay still and silent so that I'm kind of forced to focus on his face with its nose that appears to have been broken at least once in the past and the dark blue eyes that are not, in fact, twinkling with humour but glistening with disappointment, disgust even. It's that look he has that tells small children and grown-ups alike: 'I know you've been naughty.' There is something about him, 'The Principal', as he refers to himself (although he told me on first meeting, 'Just call me Steve'), that makes me feel like a schoolboy. Of course, I have some idea of what he experienced himself as a schoolboy because he comes from the same country as me, a foreign land so fractured that once you leave it you feel free to reinvent yourself. Because who really knows the truth about what happened there? And even if anybody did, the likelihood is that they too would be trying to leave the past behind them.

But Steve is not like that. He talks openly about Zimbabwe. 'I can't believe we grew up in the same place,' he says. 'I wonder what the people back home would think of us now.' And then he gives me that look. And I want to say to him: 'Okay, Steve, I get the message.' It's something along the lines of: 'Be sure your sins will find you out.' As if he has nothing to hide, nothing to be ashamed of, himself.

The street seems very dark although there are halos around the streetlamps and some pale security lights on in the small, single-storey shops. They offer mending and dry-cleaning services, which no one appears to want at this early hour. The last shop in the short row abuts a high brick wall. I guess this is the wall encircling, or at least fronting, the school. I run my fingers along it, as if I'm one of its young pupils, feeling the rough bobbles of the brick under my fingertips. The wall is almost damp with cold. After about half a block, I'm relieved to see a doorframe coming up on my right.

There is a keypad with buttons. What am I meant to press? But then I see the heavy wooden door is standing wide open. I walk through the gap. On my right, a three-storey Victorian school building is almost black against the gunmetal grey sky. It's so dark, I can only just make out the white-painted window frames, each window divided into nine small panes of glass which seem to be opaque, for it is impossible to see through them. On the side of the building closest to me there is a pathetic light above a door and I head towards it. The word 'Administration' is painted in black cursive writing. I turn the handle hard, expecting it to be stiff, but it moves smoothly and opens in a rush so I almost fall into a dimly lit, carpeted room. I walk further into what seems to be a reception area and the door bangs shut behind me.

Opposite is a corridor, tunnel-like in the gloom. There are closed doors on either side and further down it becomes so black I can't tell if the corridor has ended or if the dim light simply doesn't reach any further. I expect the silence to be shattered at any moment by a flung-open door as Steve comes out of his office to meet me.

I shiver. Why the bloody hell did I agree to this meeting? But Steve on the phone, as in person, is very persuasive, charismatic even, and he kept going on in that accent I remember so well. And he was desperate: 'Please, man, come see me in the morning. It's gotta be before school, hey? And it has to be you, Ian, do you get me? It has to.'

So I walk forwards, down the dark corridor, and there is just enough light to make out the letters painted on each door. 'Secretary' I read on one, 'Bursar' on another. I squint through the darkness at the last door, dead ahead of me. 'Principal's Office'. Putting down my heavy briefcase, I knock in a jaunty sort of way. No answer.

I can't hear a sound. It's as if I'm in an underground cavern. Maybe Steve's off having a pee. I knock again. Surely he's not late, the complete bloody bastard. I imagine Lara stretching as she wakes in my bed. Man, I long to be at home again. I'm so peeved I grab at the door handle with quite unnecessary force. The door opens quickly and I'm blinded by a beam of light, the sun piercing through the morning cloud at last, and shining through the large picture window at the back of the room. Behind the dark silhouette of the Principal's giant desk his chair has swung sideways. In front of the chair, as if ejected from it, lies a body.

I take in a breath, feel my stomach fizz. Every instinct tells me to step back. My training compels me to step forward. I put a foot in front of me and sort of half-crouch like a tennis player waiting for the serve. I am ready, fight or flight, I could go either way. But nothing happens. There is only the sound of my own breathing, harsh and rapid.

As my eyes adjust to the light, the body starts to take on the wide-shouldered, slightly paunchy figure of a man who played rugby in his youth and still drinks beer in his middle-age. In my heart, I know already. This is Steve. Is he dead? His eyes are still open, matt blue like the Indian Ocean. A hirsute man, his cheeks bear traces of evening shadow. The professional in me wonders how long he's been here. His mouth sags open. I can smell the rusty aroma of blood but can't see any. I take a tentative step closer, tell myself it's not Steve, just another one of the very many corpses I've seen in my life. The body's arm is up next to the face, protecting it perhaps? I should see if there's a pulse. But as I look closer at the head, I see there is no need, for the back of the skull has been smashed, the black hair matted with blood and gobbets of flesh.

I walk backwards, still facing the room, until I am again standing in the doorway of Steve's office. I keep my eyes on the body lying on the carpet but I deliberately don't blink so that my eyesight becomes blurry and I don't have to keep seeing Steve's features. Then I take out my mobile, tap in a number. 'Greta, this is DCI Ian Botes. Get me Inspector Clarke.'

'DI Clarke, sir.' Dave Clarke's familiar chirpy voice in my ear.

I talk rapidly into the phone: 'Dave, I'm at the London School of Nations. I've got a body: white male, early forties, believed to be the principal, Steve Duggan.' I pause. 'Smashed skull.' I snap the phone shut. Dave Clarke and I have worked together for nearly three years now; extended explanations are unnecessary. He knows what needs to be done when a body is found although usually, of course, I am not the person who actually finds it. My presence here is something I *will* have to explain to Dave.

My eyes focus again on Steve's body lying in front of me in a pool of blood and brains. Man, it's unbelievable. The last time I saw this guy he was so *alive*. I make myself take a deep breath; I'm a bloody professional, for Pete's sake, and I could really use the fact that I'm first on the scene. So I walk, slowly and carefully, and crouch down next to the body. I want to look more closely at the head wound but my gaze is caught by Steve's face; by those blue eyes stuck open but sightless. As I stare into them, my memory superimposes an image of the laughing expression he used to wear, the one that radiated good humour and hail-fellow-well-met ebullience, that masked completely the sort of man he really was.

I am jolted by a sudden noise. It's the closing of a door. I am aware again that it is still very early in the morning and I am here alone with a corpse. Or, maybe not alone. I make myself turn around slowly and look down the long, dark corridor that led me to Steve's room. Oh, man. There is a figure standing just inside the main entrance, the one I half-dived through what seems like an eternity ago.

It's way too soon for SOCOs to have arrived and yet the figure I see is dressed in overalls zipped to the neck and, slowly, carefully, he is pulling on rubber gloves, paying great attention to ensuring each finger is perfectly sheathed.

The silence continues around me. I can hear my own heartbeat. I think suddenly of the advice game-rangers give: should you see an elephant charging towards you, don't, whatever you do, run. Just stay still. And as the tanned ranger is saying this, deadly earnest, you're thinking sure, man, no problem, if an enormous elephant is thundering towards me, tusks lowered, you know what? I will just stand there. Yeah, right. I feel the same now. I really, really want to run. But I make myself size up the enemy.

He appears huge to me: six and a half foot at least and his overalls pulled tight around a massive torso as he looks down at his gloved fists, which he is slowly and methodically clenching then uncurling. Slowly he looks up. He is wearing goggles which are white – starkly, clinically so – and have reflective lenses. I can't see his eyes or tell if he can see me. He starts to do a kind of jog on the spot. It reminds me of how the riot police back in Africa used to psych themselves up before they charged in to disperse the crowd. He starts mumbling something. His voice gets louder but I still can't hear clearly through the thudding in my ears. Is he counting? And then suddenly he stops: both the counting and the manic jogging, stands still. I guess he's seen me. We face each other like two animals in the wild, sizing each other up, weighing our options. My back is against the wall, so to speak, so my only option is to fight. Or, given that he is huge and dressed for a slaughterhouse, to beg for mercy. But he's standing close to the door that leads to the outside so he has more choices. Incredibly slowly, he reaches behind himself, pulls open the door and backs out through it. He lets go of the door, turns and runs. The door slams shut.

'Stop! Police!' I shout. I can be very brave once the danger has passed. I often wonder when I will be caught out and someone will recognise that I am a terrible coward. I start to run after him, fling open the door, and burst out into the frosty morning.

He has set a course directly across the playing fields, away from the buildings. To my right, I see Dave Clarke and a uniform come in through that door in the wall that's been left wide open. 'Dave! That one!' I point to the running figure; he is closer to them than to me. They both give chase. Mr Overalls is running towards a line of trees. Straight-backed, his legs pumping rhythmically, he looks like an automaton on a set course. Our uniform, young and fast, comes up on Mr Overalls' flank and brings him down with a flying tackle. He grimly holds on to the legs trying to immobilise the booted feet but Mr Overalls is fighting ferociously and rears up on powerful forearms. Dave slams his body down across Mr Overalls' shoulders and I rush in to help grapple with his flailing arms until we have them behind his back and we can cuff the gloved wrists.

Mr Overalls has no chance now. And it's as if he realises that, for he becomes still, only his mouth continuing to move, mumbling.

'What's he saying?' Uniform asks the obvious question. But I can't make it out. Mr Overalls is lying on the grass in a foetal position and I bend my head down so that my ear is closer to his mouth. He's not as young as I first thought – could be mid-thirties – with a neat blond moustache above moist lips. And now I can hear it. It's the same thing, over and over, becoming each time clearer and louder. He is repeating a string of numbers: 'three-one-five-four-seven-two-nine-six'.

His voice rises to a shout, 'THREE-ONE-FIVE-FOUR-SEVEN-TWO-NINE-SIX!' and I rear back from him. The tendons in his neck are standing out and there is spittle on his cheeks and between his teeth as he screams.

2

'Stop it! Stop! Leave him alone.'

I look up from the man, curled in foetal position, shouting numbers, to see a woman running towards us, lurching and stumbling in her heeled brown boots. Her tan woolly coat is flapping in the wind and her handbag swings back and forth as she runs.

'Leave him alone,' she repeats to no one in particular. She goes to the man lying on the grass, hunches down beside his head, puts a hand on his shoulder. 'Dan, are you all right?' Close up, her hair is mostly covered by a brown woolly hat. She wears no make-up or earrings, only an expression somewhere between irritation and contempt.

The man doesn't answer but stops shouting and even though he presses his lips together, they are clearly trembling.

I step forward, put my arm out to help her up. She ignores it. I speak quietly: 'Miss, I am Detective Chief Inspector Botes.'

This brings her to her feet. She faces me, gestures towards the large figure in overalls lying shaking on the grass. 'What has he done?'

'I don't know yet. He ran from the scene.'

'The scene of what?'

I have no intention of explaining to an unknown woman in the middle of a school playing field in the freezing cold. So I continue as if she hasn't spoken. 'You must have heard what he was shouting. Did you recognise the phone number?'

She looks at me closely. 'It's not a phone number, Constable.' I don't correct her on my title, although she has stripped me of several ranks. I just wait, let a silence grow between us. I look away from her and nod to Dave Clarke, still standing beside the man she called Dan who lies on the grass, not saying anything but with spittle hanging from his mouth and his whole body quivering with tension. Dave says something quietly in the ear of the PC kneeling next to Dan and then walks off in the direction of the administration building to meet the SOCOs. 'It's his army number.' The woman beside me speaks at last.

'What?'

'The number he's been shouting. It's his army number, what they used to call a serial number. Dan's not been the same since he came back from Helmand. They call it post-traumatic stress. If he gets a terrible fright or shock, he repeats his army number over and over again. He's had an attack like this before.'

'Do you know who to call when it happens?'

'I have the number of his psychiatric nurse. I'll go and get it from my office.' She turns to walk towards the school building but stops when she sees all the activity there. SOCOs are in and out of the wedged-open door to administration. Uniformed officers are standing at the main entrance creating a human barrier against the parents and children arriving for school. The woman starts walking again so I have to put a detaining hand on her arm. 'I'm afraid you can't go in there.'

'Why?' She is not being confrontational; her tone is wary and her voice hesitant as if she's not really sure she wants to ask the question.

Again, I don't answer. I am considering where to take her for questioning when she says: 'It's Steve, isn't it?'

'Steve?' As if I don't know who Steve Duggan is. 'What makes you think that?'

And now she looks at me with derision in her eyes. I still find myself surprised sometimes when people are not scared of the police. Back in Zimbabwe I saw an old guy wet himself when the police told him to get off his bicycle. And then later, well, you could never really be sure what the police would do next. But this is England. The rule of law applies even to the law itself. It's civilised. None the less, a few metres away there is the body of a man who has been bashed so hard he's wearing his brains in his hair. *Plus ça change* as they say in France.

My phone rings in my pocket. 'Excuse me,' I say, 'I have to take this.' The woman looks uninterested. I take the phone out of my pocket and look at the caller ID. It's the other woman in my life: my sister, Jackie.

'Hey, Ian.'

'Jackie. To what do I owe the pleasure?'

'I wanted to see if you're free for dinner tonight. I'm making babotie.'

I look over at the school building and my deputy, Dave, comes out of the entrance, makes eye contact and starts walking towards me. 'Things are hectic at the moment.' Realising I sound ungracious, I add, 'But I'll let you know by midday, okay?'

I turn my back to Dave, speak quietly into the phone: 'Hey, Jackie, have you heard of a guy called Steve Duggan? He's from the homeland.'

There is a silence but I haven't got time to wait it out.

'Jackie?'

'A Steve Duggan was at school with me, for A-levels. In Banket. After you left.' A brief moment of excitement gives way to a feeling of apprehension. Duggan and my sister knew each other? I know better than to let Jackie realise I'm worried by her revelation. 'Great,' I say, 'I'll ask you about him at dinner tonight.'

'So you *are* coming?'

I wouldn't miss it for the world now.

THOMAS WATSON
The Regimental Boxer

FROM THE DOORWAY I studied the four hundred uniformed souls packed into the gymnasium for Guardsman Petersen's first bout. The crowd was no surprise – the regimental boxing always proved popular, for it was the sole occasion in the calendar when a man from the ranks could strike an officer and receive honourable congratulations. But this year's attendance seemed markedly impressive. Prime vantage points in the hall and on the balcony had been keenly contested by the men who were hopeful for a bruising contest, though few seats would prove better than my own. You see things differently from the cornerpost. You see a lot that others, even the judges, may miss: a grimace, a low blow, the giveaways.

Alone under the lights the referee stood and squinted, awaiting the boxer's arrival. We entered together, Petersen and I, accompanied by the fanfare of a single drummer who escorted us towards the raised platform illuminated in the centre of the gym. I kept one hand on Petersen's shoulder as we passed row upon row of men in combat fatigues, seated on foldaway chairs. Seeing us, they rose and applauded, drowning out the staccato burst of the drum roll with their shouts of encouragement. They cheered for Petersen as they had done for Hardy the previous year.

Approaching ringside, the Guardsmen gave way to senior ranked officers in full dress, seated on comfortable chesterfields. Major Galbraith flicked us the deftest of nods as Petersen climbed the few steps up to the platform and slipped between the ropes. In the brutal glare of the rudimentary spotlights, it became impossible to see beyond the dimensions of the ring. The ropes became a threshold beyond which a darkness began. From the darkness came jeers as the white-shirted announcer introduced our opponent. I took position at my post and watched on at ankle level as Captain Lacey entered the ring. The referee gave his brief pre-fight instructions and the two fighters readied themselves. Beneath their soft footfalls the blue canvas creaked. The honour of three soldiers hung in the balance.

At the opening bell the fighters approached and tapped gloves. Petersen adopted his stance, Lacey did likewise and the first of three Queensbury-governed rounds was underway. Lean, wiry and with a three-inch height advantage, the Captain went straight in, sticking his jab on the Guardsman before waltzing out of reach. Petersen hunkered, bull-like, keeping his chin tucked and his guard up. Once more Lacey came at him, attempting to work some room between our boy's forearms, but the Guardsman stayed compact and resisted his inclination to brawl. Sweat glistened and flowed across his hunched shoulders, threatening to smudge his coarsely drawn tattoos – the visible souvenirs of idle time in desert camps and mess tents. Petersen weathered the advance and the partisan crowd raised its voice as one in countenance.

The Captain pivoted and held the centre of the ring, dominating it with the same lofty sense of entitlement that was all too common among the young captains of the regiment. With thirty seconds to go in the round, Lacey ducked under Petersen's flailing hook. Locking eyes with mine, he smirked. How I wanted to shake off my creaking knees, to part the ropes and test exactly how well stitched this box-ticker was. When a card like Captain Lacey comes up, a longing rises in me, a judicious desire to dust off the old sixteen-ouncers and see what these arms have left in them. But as much as I would have enjoyed letting loose my own right hand upon Lacey's jaw, this was the Guardsman's fight. It was Petersen's duty to poke at the seams, to find the fraying strands of the Captain's integrity and pick them loose.

*

Petersen had knocked on my door one late summer day in 1945, and asked me, Marlowe, the old man of the battalion, to train him. I suppose it was my reputation that brought him to me. I had developed a knack for barking instructions at naïve young men in my quarter of a century as Company Sergeant Major, and boxing was in my blood all right. My pa and uncles had all enjoyed brief successes in their day, prior to the Great War. Perhaps Petersen had heard of my own exploits in the ring of the hiding I gave Major Galbraith almost a decade ago, back when I too held the rank of Guardsman. Or maybe he had seen me in Hardy's corner the year before and was simply compelled to keep that link alive.

He cut straight to it, outlining his intent to enter the annual competition as a light heavyweight. I admit I was sceptical. He didn't have the build of a boxer and I thought he'd make a more natural heavyweight. Back then, he seemed nothing more than an overweight Guardsman looking to lose a little around the gut; I didn't realise that it was the prospect of facing Captain Lacey that drove him.

It didn't take long to see that what he lacked on the technical side he made up for in heart – and that was something you couldn't be taught. We agreed to meet by the bandstand, Hyde Park, at O-seven-hundred. I was ten minutes early and there he was shadow boxing with the morning sun low at his back, his crude silhouette stretched twenty-five meters over the dew-laden grass. I set him laps and round and round the Round Pond he had gone. Three minutes on, one minute off. 'Now go again,' I'd said. 'And this time get yourself round in two-ten.'

And so our sessions took shape: circuits, rope work, conditioning, then weights, pad work, sparring and on it went. After each drill, he'd ask, 'What next, Sir?' and set right to it. We started with two sessions a day, wrapping up each one with a series of punishing sprints along Birdcage Walk. Although this often left him broken and in bits, he'd always show up the next day ahead of time. I'd come out at Buckingham Gate and find him there, shadow boxing, working on his jab and his big left hook.

That was the thing about Petersen, he never skimped and he never held anything back, not like some knuckleheads. Some guys, you train them all morning long and it's as though they are keeping a lid on the venom, or perhaps they lack it entirely. You have to be sly and tell them that every other drill is the last of the day. Not with Petersen though.

He was in a different class. He had the correct makeup, the right temperament from the get-go: courage and the quiet inner strength to step inside the ropes and do himself and his brother Guardsman justice. As fight night drew near, it was at his request that we upped his training to three sessions a day. The weight fell from his frame like autumn leaves.

Petersen's superiors confirmed my impression of the lad. He'd come through the war with dignity, a credit to the regiment. I didn't need to ask them about Captain Lacey. You get a good measure of things as a non-commissioned officer – odd snippets reach even the most unlikely corners. I'd heard how on the arduous approach to the Mareth Line, he had farmed out his seat in the lead convoy vehicle, nominating a Guardsman to ride in his place as he slunk back to a spot in the safety of the column. And yet he was up for promotion, a fact that implied his timorousness had been missed, or outright ignored, by the senior ranked officers. His father's efforts at Ypres were deemed more relevant in his case for advancement.

That this fainthearted man could be a proficient pugilist seemed to violate some natural order. But he did possess some strengths, and he trained to these, few though they were. In Lacey's case, as long as he had a height advantage, or could hold the centre of the ring, he could come out on top over three rounds. But while he moved reasonably well and was skilled at evading a punch, his own were not so fierce. He got by on arrogance and bravado. It was all part of his camouflage; he bore all the markings of a fearsome opponent but if you stripped him of his swagger and his rank, you would see that he lacked the necessary venom to inflict a decisive blow. Rarely did he attack with power, favouring instead a controlled, measured style, keeping half an eye on the judge's table.

*

The bell rang for the second round. Petersen began to get his shots off and fired his jab. He kept his right cocked, ready to deliver should his opponent's guard slip. But Lacey's defence was steadfast. He peered at Petersen over the top of his red gloves, elbows kept in tight to his body as he held the centre of the ring. Petersen stepped in and threw successive lefts. The taller man leaned back, avoiding the jab, and countered. He stepped in off his back foot, launched a left of his own, and another, hissing with every punch. 'Usss. Usss – usss.'

Petersen parried the advance but twisted too far to his right, and Lacey punished this error with a swift hook to the cheek. The crowd winced at the sound of the impact as the Guardsman momentarily appeared vulnerable. It was the first time I had seen him take such a hit and I was relieved to see he quickly regained his composure. My pa would have said he had a great set of whiskers to carry on from a hook like that – and whiskers, like heart, could not be taught. At the table to my left the three judges marked their cards according to rank.

The blow had caused Petersen's head guard to come loose, blocking his peripheral vision. The protective gear could be as cumbersome as a ceremonial bearskin – he did well to resist the urge to adjust it as he moved forward, weaving beneath Lacey's parries.

'Ten seconds to go. Unleash!' I shouted.

Now tiring and faced with Petersen's left, Lacey struggled to keep his guard up, as though he had kettle bells tied to his elbows. Petersen stepped in again, jabbed and usurped control of the centre of the ring. Jab-jab-right and Lacey was on the ropes. With nothing left in his arms or legs and only five seconds in the round to go, the Captain grabbed Petersen in a clinch, muffling the punches. Behind me the crowd responded with boos and jeers. It was a dirty move, making the Guardsman take his weight like that.

The referee had to come between the boxers at the end of the round and peel Lacey off. I slipped between the ropes and stepped into the ring as Petersen walked back to the corner, eyeing Lacey all the while. I sat him down against the padded ring post and with haste I stepped in to his eye-line, removed his gum shield, and lifted his chin. I poured a little water into his mouth, raising the bucket in time for him to spit.

'Leave that bloody headgear alone. For Christ's sake, focus.' I figured he needed a little bite. 'And get your gloves off the ropes. Don't let that rat see you tire.'

His vest was soaking and it clung to his chest, which rose and fell away as he filled his lungs.

'Jab's looking good, Petersen,' I continued. 'Double up on the jab. And when he comes for you with those lefts, you keep your head moving, stay on your toes and counter. He's getting lazy with those elbows.'

Petersen lifted his chin and I adjusted the strap on the head-guard. I wasn't sure if any of my chatter was making a mark; he looked through me – the sort of look I had seen on the faces of men as they huddled in trenches and fixed bayonets.

I thought back to the Friday before the fight. With a few hours' leave, I had taken Petersen to a pub on Petty France. He chose a small table in one corner of the saloon bar and we huddled over our pints, talked tactics, and considered our opponent's weaknesses.

'The key to unlocking a fighter like Lacey,' I had said, 'is to surprise him, present him with an unknown. Hardy proved that when he floored him with his right.'

Petersen just sat and stared at his pint.

'What is it?' I asked him. 'What is it about Lacey?'

'Lacey came back,' he said. He took a sip of beer and wiped the froth from his upper lip. 'Too many better men didn't. Hardy didn't.'

'*Ten seconds*,' shouted the referee.

I resumed my ringside duties with urgency. 'Last round, make it count.' I wiped the sweat from Petersen's face and from his gloves and stuck a thick glob of Vaseline to the welt that was forming under his eye. 'Three minutes. It's all you need. You're in better shape. Use your feet. Move-move-move. Get in close, watch and wait and then when he lets you in for a sniff, you punish him.' I crashed a fist into my open palm.

'Here, get some more water in you.' He cocked his head back and drank. I slipped his gum-shield back into his mouth and he bit down, contorting his face into a snarl. 'Don't blow it, son!' I said. 'Don't make it personal.'

Petersen stood and looked at me. 'Everything's personal, Marlowe,' he grunted through the gum-shield as he slapped his gloves together.

'*Seconds out.*'

I slipped through the ropes and hopped off the raised platform. Turning back to reach for the stool, I watched Petersen limber up, rolling his shoulders. The referee vacated the centre of the ring as the bell sounded. Guardsman and Captain advanced for one final round.

Shouts from the ranks drowned out my own instructions. 'Give it to him, Petersen,' they yelled. 'Give him the hell he deserves.' The Guardsman crossed the barren canvas and approached his mark. In the glare of the overhead lights there was no place for a shadow to hide. He circled and stalked, patiently waiting for Lacey to give himself away.

A minute into that final round, the Guardsman seized upon a chance. Lacey retreated under Petersen's jab, attempted to counter with his left and followed up with a tired right. It was an aimless punch – Petersen slipped it with ease and the Captain's gloved hand hung, useless in the void.

The Guardsman went all in, he was the fitter of the two by far – the sprints up and down Birdcage Walk had seen to that. He landed with his left. Once, twice, with a volley of blows on to the nose and then chin, Lacey's head snapped back. The Captain attempted to steady himself against the ropes, but his breathing was wasteful and he snatched at thin air.

'You've got him now, Petersen!' 'His knees are going!' The shouts rose to a roar over my shoulder as Lacey's defensive punches lost all coordination. I slammed the canvas with the palms of my hands, urging our boy on.

The Captain flung another wild right that left his lower body unguarded. Petersen ducked beneath the haymaker, stepped off his right to realign his body and planted his left foot forward. With his base set, he targeted the gap between his opponent's elbow and ribs; I saw the punch before he threw it. A dip of his knee set the mechanics in motion: momentum corkscrewed upwards through his body, from his hips via his breadbasket, across his shoulders and down his left arm, doglegged at the elbow. The hook tore in to the right side of the Captain's torso, sending ripples through his flesh. Lacey's knee buckled and he crumpled to the deck.

The referee was over him, counting out on his fingers. 'One . . . two . . . three . . .' Lacey began to stir as Petersen bounced on his toes in the neutral corner. 'Four . . . five . . . six . . .'

It wasn't quite enough.

On 'eight' Lacey pulled himself off the canvas, the referee checked him over and the fight resumed. You could see he had nothing left in him, from the manner in which he kept on grappling to stifle Petersen's incoming attacks. The referee didn't intervene, and Lacey saw the round out that way.

*

In the locker room afterwards Petersen sat with his head bowed as I cut him out of his wraps and inspected his bloated hands. The crowd was muted as the final bout of the evening got under way – their shouts came to us as faint echoes. As I strapped ice packs to Petersen's swollen knuckles, I eulogised that left hook. What a hit it was: clean and smooth, from the heart as much as from the hips, the kind of body shot you play over and over in your mind. It was an uncompromising punch of which Hardy would have been proud. Petersen, though, stayed silent as I talked on.

I often think back to that moment when the Captain's arm was raised to victory. It was a shambolic decision, the kind that would have set off a riot among the punters at York Hall. Even the referee looked embarrassed about it. The men sat in stunned disbelief, and as the realisation spread, catcalls emanated from the dark recesses of the gymnasium, while Major Galbraith and the men of senior rank clapped on politely. And that's how it plays out sometimes, especially in the army. Lacey gets a write-up in the back pages of *Guards Magazine* and his name on a plaque, while Petersen returns to the dull anonymity of ceremonial duties.

There are winners in name, those with titles and accolades; and then there are those who live as we all might dream: the best of us who never see the parade. For these men, victory rests in the method, in rising to a challenge and meeting it head on with dignity and polished brass buttons. To act without honour and good grace would defile their integrity, leave their salt sullied and a brackish taste in the mouth. *History is written by the winners*, that's what we are told, isn't it, while truth, truth lies cut adrift in no man's land, in tales unfermented by official verdicts and party lines. In the stories of Guardsmen Petersen and Hardy it flickers on, a dying beacon in the gathering night.

JOANNA ROSENTHALL
A Child Dies

ROSIE FELT IN ABSOLUTE CONTROL speeding through the London night. She must stay clear-headed. The street lights had turned the shop-fronts into glassy reflective screens which were mesmerising. She put her foot down a fraction harder on the accelerator and felt the resistance in the steering wheel. The route was hard-wired into her. Right here, left at the lights, then straight on . . . The police had stopped her before, on this very same journey in the dead of night. She always had the sentence ready – I'm a doctor on the way to a child who's dying – and no policeman dared to hold her up. Sometimes she'd had to flash her ID, but it was always quick. No one wanted to be responsible for something like that. She realised that she felt the same. She didn't want to be responsible either. But she was the doctor. She had no choice.

The only person at the nurses' station was sour Irene, whom none of the children liked. She was bending low over her notes, laboriously writing something. Why couldn't she just look up and say hello?

'Hi Irene,' Rosie said, trying to force a little warmth into her voice, slowing her pace but not stopping.

Irene looked up, her eyes still squinting from her work. Her forehead seemed deep and taut, her hair hidden beneath her cap. 'It's good you're here,' she said drily. 'They're too young, the registrars on duty tonight.'

Rosie said nothing. She didn't want to agree or disagree. It was true, but they'd all had to do it at that age. Irene just wanted to complain.

She went quickly to the small cupboard of a room where the staff each had a grey metal locker. She took off her coat and hung it on the peg inside hers, reluctant to part with her warm layers. She peeled her jumper off. This was the moment when she tended to talk to herself, just quietly in whispers. She often felt a little surprised by what came out. Sometimes she called for her mother. 'Mum . . . Mum . . .' although at other times she found herself speaking irritably, 'Oh Mum,' as if she was accusing her mother of something. She quickly put on her scrubs – they smelt strongly of something chemical and felt cold and empty.

She washed her hands carefully, thoroughly, even though she was in a hurry. And then she was ready. She didn't hesitate. She went straight to the bed where Sally was lying on her back, naked except for a pair of hospital paper pants, an incontinence pad bulking them out. Isabelle, one of the nurses, was tenderly sponging her down.

Before the treatment Sally had wonderful dark, looping curls. They became wet and thin when she was unwell, and lay in dank lifeless clumps. Then with startling speed, after the chemo, they'd fallen out until the wispy long strands had looked so strange that the nurse had prompted her mother to shave off the rest. Her mother had come in the next day with an electric ladies' shaver in a feminine shade of mauve. Rosie had stared, watching the mother standing over the child's head, one hand holding it still and the other guiding the shaver in sweeping lines. The whirr of the electricity, the painful baldness of the scalp. The mother had done the job gently and perfectly, going over and over until Sally's skin was entirely exposed. Rosie had still been watching as the mother peered at the razor, switched it off and then leant forward. She didn't kiss the top of her daughter's skull, as Rosie had expected, instead she moved her lips all over the exposed head as if she was a baby herself, getting to know something with her mouth. Rosie had turned away.

The bald children were invisible on that ward; there were so many of them.

But that was a year ago, when they'd all been full of hope. Now, things were bad. One of Sally's lungs had already collapsed earlier in the night. That wasn't unusual with this illness and it had happened many times before. But now the other lung seemed in danger of going as well and her oxygen level kept nose-diving. That was why the registrar had phoned, and why Rosie had immediately heard fear in the young doctor's voice. In the middle of the lengthy explanation of all the tests, Rosie had interrupted her.

'Do you want me to come?' She heard the impatience in her own voice. Why couldn't they just ask her from the start, 'Can you come?' It would make it easier. Instead there was this long-drawn-out game where she felt she was supposed to be saving their pride.

'Yes,' the young woman said instantly, 'that would be good.' Her relief was palpable and Rosie too felt relieved.

'The parents know. We decided to wake them.' The young woman was whispering down the phone as if she and Rosie and were now conspirators.

'That's good,' Rosie wanted to use the registrar's name but it had slid without warning down a little chute in her mind. Perhaps she wasn't so cool herself, even after all these years. 'Listen, you've done everything you should have done.'

'Yes. I know.' The young woman's voice still sounded small down the line but Rosie could hear that she was trying to re-establish herself as the doctor she was meant to be.

Rosie had wanted to add, 'People do die, you know. You can't save everyone.' She was surprised at the heat of anger that surfaced and she stopped herself. She'd hated it when positions had been reversed and some consultant had said the same to her.

Right at the start of this call Rosie knew she'd go. If a registrar calls like that you can't leave them. They knew all the theory but handling it without a senior person there was too tough. They really did look like kids not that long out of school, and here they were with people's lives in their hands. They did their best not to call. But anyway, this was Sally. Rosie wanted to be there.

Rosie had felt a personal attachment to Sally right from the first meeting, a year ago now. At that time, Sally had already been in hospital for five months. She'd been under the care of another consultant who was going away on maternity leave, so she was transferred to Rosie's list. She had seen the child on the ward before and had even said hello a couple of times, but Rosie was not prepared for how she would feel when she sat on the edge of Sally's bed.

'I'm your new doctor, Sally, and I'm going to do the best I can . . .' she'd started.

'I hate doctors,' Sally said.

Rosie nodded. 'I can understand that,' she said, 'I know you just want to be at home and better.'

'Can you make me better?' Sally asked, although this was less of a plea and more of a demand, 'The other one didn't seem to be able to.'

Rosie had been stunned into silence. No other child had ever spoken to her in this way.

She reached out and squeezed Sally's hand, 'I'll do my best.' Sally had stared in an awful unseeing way. Rosie wanted to hold her, to squeeze life and health into her. What could she say? Sally was utterly still but there was something about the child that made Rosie know she was waiting to see if this new person was the one who could bring her back to the right side of the line.

'Of course I'll try my best. I'll really, really try,' Rosie said, and the girl had nodded. But when Rosie stood up to leave, Sally's eyes were still dull and flat, staring at her.

'I have to leave now,' Rosie said. She was used to children tugging at her white coat, 'I'll come back when I get a moment.'

Rosie was almost at the next bed, when she heard Sally's voice calling after her.

'I'm cold,' she said, but what Rosie heard was, 'Don't leave me.'

Rosie turned, 'You could do with a little woolly cap, I'll ask the nurse to bring you one.'

'They're scratchy,' Sally said, not looking up. Her arms were crossed and Rosie noticed how small and sharp her elbows were.

'Well, that's given me something to think about.' Rosie returned to Sally's bed, 'Why don't you wear one for the time being, just to keep you warm, and I'll keep thinking about what would suit you. A special hat, just for you. Leave it with me,' she said.

For a moment Sally's eyes melted a little as Rosie steadily held her gaze. I'm going to knit her one myself, she thought. I'm going to go to a wool shop and I'm going to buy the softest, most beautiful yarn I can lay my hands on and knit her a beautiful little hat.

Afterwards Rosie had realised that she felt this child was special because she was so angry and didn't see the need to protect anyone from her feelings. Her lip was permanently curled in furious resentment. When she'd been able to walk, she'd stomped about the ward, and when she couldn't get out of bed, she'd smouldered. Rosie wanted to make Sally better. She had never felt it with such an acute lick of pain before.

*

At first Rosie thought she'd got the wrong bed. Sally didn't look like Sally. Her face was bloated and lumpy, and the crouching elderly figures leaning over her were the wrong parents. Surely they hadn't sent the grandparents?

The doctor who'd phoned was at her side almost immediately.

'I'm so glad you're here,' she was still whispering. Rosie made a mental note. She must tell Claire – the registrar's name had suddenly popped back into her mind – that if she was saying things that needed whispering, she should save them for later. It would make everyone more nervous if they heard the doctors whispering.

'I'm pleased to have come,' Rosie said out loud. 'Now show me.'

She didn't have to study the charts for long to know that Sally was dangerously ill. She went through the sequence of events over the last ten days. The child had a small heart attack over a week ago, probably due to the lack of oxygen; she'd had a fracture in her spine and her leg where the overload of blood cells had accumulated and were attacking the bone. She'd been on a respirator for the last ten days. That had shown that she was deteriorating, but now, in spite of that, her oxygen level had plummeted again.

Sally's little body was giving up. She was deeply asleep in an induced coma, and that at least was a blessing. She wouldn't be suffering. Her small bony torso rose and fell, rose and fell. How natural it seemed, the steady breathing, it made everything feel safe. Rosie wanted to just stand still, not think, not move. It was the machine-like evenness of the movement up and down that was drawing her in. Rosie scanned the child's face, the bloated cheeks, the strange roughness in the skin. She shrank from seeing that beautiful long-legged girl in this state.

Emma, one of the other nurses, was changing the saline. She quickly finished the task and then stood to the side and looked at Rosie, her eyes saying, 'Do something.' She was holding her hands up, covered in bright purple latex gloves as if they might contaminate someone. People often did that to you once you were a doctor. Change this! Make the illness go away. Even the nurse couldn't bear it.

Rosie might have shrugged or shaken her head from side to side, but she didn't move. She returned the nurse's look. She raised her shoulders just a small amount, but enough to communicate. She felt a lurch of nausea. People die, she told herself. All people die. But this is Sally. She had no answer to that. She stood still in front of the child's bed. Sally was now a small shrunken figure, her skin had a greyish sheen. Large spaces had opened up between her small body and the blue plastic pads designed to stop her banging herself against the bed. She was a little bag of skin and bones surrounded by the paraphernalia of high-tech health care. If only Sally could be spared this, the same way that people take their pets to the vet so that they can slip away from all this pain into the cold, still earth.

As Rosie stood staring at the girl, suddenly so tired that she could hardly stand, she had a flash of memory. She was five, sitting in her first classroom, each child at a separate desk with a lid and a small matching chair. They were being taught to write.

'It's italics,' the teacher told them, 'Not everyone learns to write their letters like this.' Rosie felt so completely grown-up and special. In front of her she had a red-covered exercise book with lines ruled so that she could fit her letters into the spaces and knew how tall the sticks had to be. The first page was so fresh and new. The teacher had written the first letter on each line, 'a', and with careful, strained movements she was forming 'a . . . a . . . a . . .' all the way along the line. It was hard. She was on about the fifth 'a', she lifted her hand to look at what she'd done and saw she had smudged all the earlier ones as she'd moved across the page. She turned her palm over and the side of her hand was streaked with blue. She loved the smell of the ink but she wanted to cry. She couldn't do it. And then suddenly there was the sound of fluid splattering on to the floor. Rosie looked up. Water was gushing from somewhere, like a small waterfall flowing from both sides of the chair just in front of her. The girl in front didn't move or speak. Rosie stared at the grey jumper covering the girl's back. The girl was sitting upright and still, her chair standing in its own little sea of fluid. Rosie wanted to die. This shouldn't have happened here at school. Rosie was sure she had done something to make this happen. She was sure it was her fault. She didn't raise her hand. She didn't speak. Her whole body went hot. She lowered her face onto her arms in front of her as if she wanted to sleep. She could hear other children laughing and the sound of the teacher's heels coming towards her.

She pushed the memory away. She needed to be focused. Here. Now. Leaning over Sally's poor, wasted little body. It wouldn't be long now. She'd read when she was studying that when children die there's something easy about it. Adults treat it like a battle and hang on long after they should have given up. But children don't. They don't put up a fight. It had stayed in her mind. It was probably true.

She needed to talk to the parents. She mustn't put it off. She felt a swift and light efficiency take her over, always a relief. She knew what to do.

It was only when she was in the visitors' room under the bright lights that the two haunted figures turned back into Sally's parents. Sally's mother had caught her straight brown hair up in a small slide with a bow at the side of her head that looked as if it had been Sally's. She felt heat rising just under her eyes. Sally's father looked like an old man, bent and fleshless. She'd been going to explain it to them again, the respirator, the way it worked, the medically induced coma, the oxygen levels being too low, but when she saw them her capability slipped and it seemed pointless to speak.

'It's not good,' she said in the end, 'I'm sorry that's inadequate, I can explain everything if you want but I don't think there's anything else we can do. Her body's had enough and I think she's slipping away. She's comfortable, I think. She's not fighting.'

Sally's mother looked at her coldly. 'No, you can't,' she said.

Rosie felt bewildered. 'Sorry?'

'You can't explain everything. Sally's dying!' she was nearly shouting as if it was Rosie's fault. 'Do you really know that she's comfortable? You doctors make me sick.' Sally's father nudged her a little and the mother's body swayed. It was as if she was made of paper, even though her voice came out in sharp strands. Rosie recoiled. She had a sudden cold image of thrusting a knitting needle into the space where this woman's eyebrows met, in and up under the ridge of her brow. There'd be very little blood and she'd gone in an instant. Rosie stared at

Sally's mother, feeling a surge of hatred for this woman, and then equally she hated her own thoughts. Here was a woman, a mother whose child lay dying, and she wanted to attack her. Of course she couldn't explain why this was happening to Sally, a nine-year-old innocent. It didn't make any sense to anyone. She felt a kind of love for this child, but she couldn't tell them that. Sally belonged to them. Rosie knew about the dark feelings that were hard to put into words. She understood. She couldn't tell them that either. None of it could make Sally better. And that was all they wanted.

'What can I say?' she asked them, her arms swaying in front of her like lost fish, not sure what gesture they were trying to make. And then she blurted out.

'I envy you,' she said simply. 'I've not had a child. Sally is a wonderful girl. If she doesn't make it, and it looks as if she might not, you are lucky to have had her. She's very, very special.' And without looking up to see the effect she'd had, she strode out of the room, pausing briefly at the door to say that if they needed her, all they had to do was tell the nurse.

Outside, she stopped. Why had she said that? They could complain. Sally's mother seemed to be the type. She should go back and apologise. She had lost herself. She shouldn't have been telling them things about herself, not at this moment. But there it was – she'd done it. She stumbled her way to the staff night-duty room, punched out the code for the door. When she closed the door behind her it was completely dark and she couldn't see a thing after the flat glare of the corridor. She inhaled deeply. The room smelt of chemicals. She imagined that the space was so small and the door so tightly closed for days at a time, that the vinyl on the floor and the paint on the walls and the plastic on the chair seat were all slowly giving up their molecules to make a chemical soup in the air. She breathed deeply again. It had become the smell of being between one death and the next, hoping to grab a few hours' sleep before the morning. She fumbled round for the bedside lamp which was attached to the wall, to save her eyes the shock of the central light. She noticed the sound of her blind fingers, sweeping the cold wall, banging into the small wardrobe over to the left. There. She found it. She sat on the bed, made up with a thin green hospital counterpane, cold to the touch. She cradled her own head in her hands and rocked back and forth. It's okay, it's okay, she told herself out loud. I made a mistake. I am the consultant but I am human. She told herself these things over and over. Then without warning she felt a little better. She raised her head and straightened her spine. Her hands were resting in her lap.

I will go back into the ICU. I will find Sally's parents and apologise. I won't explain. I'll just say sorry. And then I will offer to stay with them in case they're afraid. I can be the doctor again.

She stood up, relieved to find she was steady on her feet. Back on the ward, Sally's parents were in the same place, on either side of Sally's bed. Bending over towards each other, their heads almost touching as if they were making a bridge over their child. The father was gently stroking the back of Sally's hand and they were both whispering to her.

Neither of them looked up but they seemed to know she had come.

'I'm so sorry for what I said earlier,' Rosie said quietly, 'I shouldn't have spoken like that.'

'Don't worry,' the father said, 'we all have a breaking point.'

'Thank you,' she said, 'I'll stay with you, if you need me here.'

'That's good,' he said. 'We both feel afraid in case something happens. We wanted you to be here. We know how much you care about Sally.'

'I'm here, and I can stay,' she said.

'We're taking it in turns,' he explained without turning away from the child, 'to tell Sally as many good memories as we can, of her life.' The mother nodded, but she didn't speak.

Rosie checked the monitors. The respirator was evenly doing its work, but Sally's heart was slowing down and irregular. It wouldn't be long. Her body was still and white, already lifeless on the bed. Rosie had a picture of Sally's little being trying to work out what to do inside the body that was giving up. Her lively little self, her angry fiery self and all of the other little bits of her had gathered together and dissolved into a small shape like the head of a pin and now this dense little shape was fading . . . receding . . . to a place of no return.

Not long after, it was time. Rosie turned to the parents. 'I could take her off the machine now, undo all the tubes and you can hold her. Hold her properly.' She didn't want to say she's gone. Sally, your daughter, has died. There was no need.

Sally's mother didn't speak, but her father nodded. He sat down quickly on a chair holding out his arms in a curve waiting for his child, as if she had come alive again. Rosie undid all the tubes, gently and swiftly, and then she scooped Sally up, careful not to let her head flop back, and laid her gently into her father's arms.

He rocked her as if she were his baby again. He sang her a song, using her name. He called out to her, 'Sally . . . Sally . . .,' as if she was lost in the garden and needed to come in now for tea. He tucked his own cheek close in to hers and then he started the whole thing again. 'I don't want to put her down,' he said. His voice was dry.

'You can be here for as long as you want,' Rosie said, wondering if she should warn them that after death the body changes, things happen which might alarm them.

'She needs a nightdress on,' Sally's father said, and Rosie was glad of a job. She would find a pretty nightdress from Sally's belongings, something that would cover up her scrawny ravaged frame.

Sally's things were all neatly folded and put in a plastic box with her name in a special storage room in the ward. She picked up the garment folded on the top. Beautiful pyjamas covered in little pink flowers, and underneath them some spotty and some stripey ones. Cheerful, comfortable garments for a little girl to love. They seemed too pretty, too bright. She chose the ones with little pink flowers, and as she lifted them, she saw the little rainbow hat that she had knitted for Sally in the softest cashmere she could find. She would take that too, to keep her head warm, she said to herself. What strange things we say and do when people die.

Sally's father had laid her on the bed. Her mother dressed her carefully, moving her limbs, and cringing away from the way her body was stiffening, becoming awkward.

'Would you like me to do it?' Rosie asked.

The mother nodded. 'She's turning blue underneath,' she wailed, 'I don't want to see her like that.' Tears began pouring from her eyes. 'I want to hold her,' she sobbed, 'but this is not my Sally. This is not my Sally.' The woman's face was ravaged with grief, huge sobs were wrenched out of her. Rosie stood there quietly and placed the palm of her hand on Sally's mother's back. She held it there firmly, feeling the sobs shaking the whole of her, then finally slowing and turning into a quieter weeping. She knew it was time for her to leave.

'You can call the nurse,' she said holding out her hand to shake each of theirs. 'She'll help you when you're ready to leave.'

CHARLOTTE EDWARDES

Aden

HERON CROSSED the hush of the Secretariat courtroom like a man condemned. He felt the starched fabric of his uniform against his skin, the weight of his formal brass buttons, a pinch from the unforgiving leather of his dress shoes. He was conscious of the line of military men watching his every step, and of the intense quiet, like a breath held.

The witness chair was to the left of Sir Harry Trusted and it struck him, as he approached it, how similar it looked to an ordinary dining room chair, one you might see in any English house, and how dwarfed and spindly and dreadfully insubstantial it was, given the weight of the evidence it had to support. When he reached it, he pulled his jacket firmly around him and sat down stiffly, as if this vessel of 'truth' was something far grander and more purposeful than it appeared.

His colleagues in the Aden Police had already delivered their evidence from this chair, at points haltingly, stumbling over their words like civilians, and then at other times recalling events fluently, as if they were back slipping in the blood of the dark streets in Crater on those dreadful nights in early December 1947.

There had been outbreaks of heckling from the military, stamped on by Sir Harry, and raised voices in the outside corridor, which the secretaries, with a clatter of heels and sharp shushing, had been quick to subdue.

Heron glanced at the rows of wooden benches ahead of him, lined with uniformed men in all manner of arrogant repose. And at the grand portraits behind them: pale and honorable men against black backgrounds, wearing expressions of superiority, the sort that went naturally with administrating a British Colony.

The courtroom silence was filled with the crack and flutter of good-quality paper being turned. There was a fit of dry coughing, and the thud of someone changing position on the bench.

The air compressed around him, stuffy and close.

He rested his hands loosely on his knee, as if at ease. He glanced at the secretaries' desk, at the group of young women sitting with piles of notepads and files and pens and pencils in pots. Paper and carbon had been wound into the typewriters, blank and ready for use. A fan fluttered dementedly in a futile bid to keep them cool.

Miss Fairley, the judge's secretary, a head-girlish air about her, stood out in her light-blue suit. Her brown hair was cropped close at the neck, not at all in the way that Pamela and the other wives wore theirs. Her face was beginning to shine in the intense heat, and he felt it too, at his temples and across the broad of his back. He wanted to wipe his neck with a handkerchief.

Sir Harry Trusted lifted his gaze from his stack of papers and, noticing that the court was assembled, he cleared his throat and looked straight at Heron with eyes that were not quite brown and not quite black. It was impossible to read either kindness or aggression in their clouded irises. The heavy, hooded lids set above his hanging jowls, topped off by the grey flaps of his wig, gave the judge the appearance of a tired old bloodhound. An old dog, Heron thought, sent from London to administer its will: the authority of Whitehall crossing seas and sands to stamp its verdict upon us.

The judge was pushing himself to his feet and stood as straight as he could in his advanced years. His pallor spoke of a harsh winter, out of place here, where most people were yellowed from years in their coastal desert. Leaning on the desk in front of him, Sir Harry opened with his formal address, as he had in the last two days of the Inquiry.

'As you all know, I have been appointed by His Excellency the Governor of Aden and the Secretary of State for the Colonies to preside over this judicial inquiry into the disturbances of last December 1947.' His voice was thick and slow and moist. 'Those disturbances saw the deaths of 37 Arabs, 82 Jews, two Indians, a Protectorate Levy, a Colony doctor and a government officer. The list of the injured runs into hundreds of names. Many have also lost their homes, businesses and possessions. This inquiry is to be held in the presence of authorised representatives of those afflicted communities.'

Heron looked around the room to acknowledge these parties by sight. He saw them nod and grumble an acknowledgement back: Mr Bentwich, a tall man with pinched features and wire spectacles, the Jewish lawyer from London; the Honourable Muhammad Salim Ali, looking splendid in his robes. He noticed now that Mr Dinshaw was looking at him with a tight smile and he returned it briefly.

The judge eased himself back into his chair and he now fixed his foggy eyes on Heron, his hands finding each other in a papery fondle.

'Captain Heron, Superintendent. We have heard the statements of some of your superior officers in the Aden Police. Now, would you kindly take us through your account of what happened on December 2nd, while you were on duty at Crater Police Station?' He looked at his notes and then at the clock high on a wall underneath the Royal Arms. Heron followed his gaze.

'I realise we won't have time to finish this morning, but take your time. Begin at the beginning and so forth. You of all people realise, of course, how important it is that we hear every detail. Do tell the court anything you might think is relevant, won't you?'

'Yes, your Honour,' Heron replied. He felt the weight of it now, the weight of British authority.

'Treacherous bastard,' he heard someone mutter in a voice he presumed was deliberately low enough to be missed by the aged judge. Heron skimmed the sneers, until he saw Colonel Burton, wearing an expression of such ill-concealed contempt that he involuntarily tensed his jaw.

Wing Commander Sykes sat beside him, the flare of red still in his cheeks, but he avoided Heron's gaze. Sykes, no longer the 'traitor': now he'd changed his evidence to suit his superiors he could sit among them as one of them.

Heron straightened in the witness chair. He felt the sweat crawl down his back like a fly. The heat tugged at his will, trying to drain the fight from him.

But he'd been waiting for this moment. The stenographer was looking up at him expectantly; Miss Fairley was beginning the neat curls of shorthand on a brand new pad. All he needed to do now was tell his story: his version of events. The truth.

Three months earlier: December 2nd 1947,
The Police Station, Crater

Crater Police Station had a distinct smell: it was the tang of Her Majesty's brown stationery, the ink of blue carbon paper, the enlivening sharpness of tobacco smoke, and that metallic zing, like a new filling, that rose from the typewriters that permanently smacked words into statements.

The whitewashed offices, like most rooms in Aden, were kept deliberately shaded, the light restrained by blinds and shutters that distorted the shadows, boxing them into uniform rectangles. Even the photographs – the obligatory line-ups of their pitifully understaffed force, in bush jackets and empire-builders: a row of bald knees and extravagant moustaches – seemed to harbour unnaturally ordered shapes.

At the front desk, the wronged, disgruntled and beleaguered jostled for the attention of the turbaned Indian staff sergeant.

Heron had been glad of this familiar bustle as he arrived at work, not just because it was provided an escape from things with Pamela, but also because he had found his brief tour of the Jewish Quarter on the way into the office unnerving.

'I mean, it's a bloody ghost town,' he remarked to Freeman and Cooper who were already in his office when he walked through the door.

There had been the usual jabber from the café speakers, broadcasting nationalist rage from Cairo, but the audience was a mere handful of white-haired men, necks bent in backgammon, and the streets around were still, as if swept by a giant unseen broom.

'A few stalls open in Section B, and the usual sullen bunch outside the Kodak shop, but barely a soul in Street 2 and Street 4.'

Freeman looked up from a charge sheet. 'A quiet Crater: always the first sign of trouble.'

He was half-sitting on Heron's desk, one buttock hitched up: a pose that would ordinarily look casual, but something about Freeman – cow-licked, elongated and sharply thin – made him look awkward.

Heron dropped his cap on the desk and poured himself coffee from the tray. He looked at the saucer holding custard creams, neatly arranged on a napkin, took one and bit into it. 'Anything last night?' he asked.

'Yup. Ten arrests, and – ' Freeman fished something out of a stack of papers and held it out to Heron.

'What is it?'

'A tip-off.'

Heron dusted the crumbs from his hands and took the envelope. They received so many of these anonymous notes at the station that it sometimes seemed that their only job was to dampen the Colony's enthusiasm for intrigue. Still, they were always worth checking.

Freeman went on: 'They're downstairs, the arrests. All coolies from up country – not one of them fazed. Actually, they seemed rather pleased to be taken down to the cells.'

The cells were beneath their feet, attached by a flight of stone stairs and a dim, narrow passage hung with the stench of ammonia and phenols.

'Food and a bed to sleep in, that's why,' Cooper said from the filing cabinet. Heron glanced at him: a folder was tucked high under his arm where he usually held his cane.

'Well, it's hardly loss of a hand, is it?' Cooper continued with a shrug. 'More like an invitation to steal than a deterrent.'

'*All* from up country?' Heron asked Freeman.

'*All*. Truckloads more arriving over night. Coolies, mostly: looking for work.'

Cooper snorted. 'Looking for trouble more like. The Colony doesn't have two pennies to rub together.' His freckled hands moved like crabs through the dividers. 'We could learn a thing or two from the Imam, you know: regular floggings, the odd amputation. These criminals would think twice if the penalty was a rather messy beheading.'

Freeman frowned: 'Cooper, you make the Nazis sound positively progressive.'

'Only to you, Freeman,' Cooper sniped with a dark look.

Heron ignored them. He was looking at the tip-off note in his hand, turning it over. Freeman started talking about the coolies again. 'Quite a number are sleeping in rock shelters outside Crater and along the road to Steamer Point.'

'They've been there a while,' Heron replied vaguely.

The envelope was addressed to him in an awkward Roman script: 'Police Heron, Crater, Aden.' It had been written by one of the cheap letter-writers in the bazaar, a spidery effort, not the expensive copper-plate of the old days. Times were hard in even in the free port.

'Anything new on the strike?' he asked the others.

'Yes. As a matter of fact Cooper and I were just about to get off and see Luqman.' Freeman leant back an inch to pick up the paper. 'He's calling it a Jewish boycott in *The Gazette* this morning. They're holding a meeting at 11 at the Ihsanullah Hotel.'

'Jewish boycott?' Heron asked. 'Oh Christ, not this again.'

'Yup.' Freeman skimmed the paper. 'But Sheikh Zubeidi is on board, Khalifa, Yafari. Oh, and Sheikh Abdullah. Those seem to be the official organisers, at any rate.'

'Yes, yes. A number of them went to see the Chief Secretary yesterday about a general strike, but "Jewish boycott"? Jesus. No wonder Crater is dead.'

'And this morning we had a complaint from the Hindu shopkeepers,' Freeman added. 'They're being intimidated to join in the strike.'

Heron stiffened. 'Is that so? Well, we need to stamp out this bloody nonsense before it takes root.'

He thought of his conversation with Ingram at the Club a few nights earlier – the older man stabbing his slabs of chips into tomato sauce as Heron talked. 'And after January I don't think we can afford to take any risks with another strike. We need to be fully prepared. If anything tensions are worse than they were a year ago.'

'Well, you know the situation better than anyone, old boy,' Ingram had said, wiping his chin with a paper napkin and signalling for another beer. 'But I know the Chief Secretary and the DC, they get frightfully antsy about budgets and they don't like to stir anti-British feeling. But, tell you what, send me a memo on it and I'll see what I can do.'

The drawer of the filing cabinet slammed shut and Cooper turned to face them.

'A civilised government would make the strike illegal,' he said. 'Ban it before the trouble starts.'

Heron shook his head. 'Not according to the District Commissioner. He thinks a ban would only encourage the wretched nationalists to go against us. He and the Governor have a notion that a peaceful protest against Palestine, with us looking on, will be good for British relations.'

Cooper made a noise of disgust. 'Like some sort of ruddy May Day parade, you mean? It's a shame the DC and the Governor don't spend more time down here in the heat of Crater, instead of at lunch parties up at Steamer Point. I can't help feeling – '

'Yes, all right, Cooper,' Heron interrupted. 'We know how you feel.' He'd noticed Freeman raise an eyebrow of approval. United only in dissent, these two.

He began to open the tip-off note, unfolding it carefully to ensure nothing was tucked inside. The paper was mottled by grease – probably the curried goat on the fingers of its author as he hurried furtively down Zafran Street, clutching it in the dusty twill of his pocket.

Inside the letter-writer had made more effort, an indulgent Arabic flourish here and there, and the note had been given a title: 'Warning.'

'There is a plot to riot against the British and Jews on account of Palestine,' it announced. 'Many will join. These are loafers, riff-raff and other foreign elements. Be warned: there is great danger in Aden.'

It ended: 'From your most loyal servant, Arab, peace-loving.'

And then in a somewhat defensive postscript, was a line in Arabic: 'The writer is writing this, though against his own Arab people, for the sake of humanity and peace for the country.'

Heron looked at the back and then at the home-made envelope. There was no lead to follow, no names. Nothing concrete. It was useless, but it stirred his existing sense of unease.

'Anything?' Freeman asked.

'Another warning of coming violence,' Heron replied. 'I get the nasty feeling the DC and the Governor are missing something here.'

He moved round his desk and sat down, putting the note on the table in front of him. 'I'll get on to Ingram. I think we ought to be on standby. And the Armed Police too.'

Cooper was wearing an I-told-you-so expression; Freeman looked uncomfortable.

'Get off to those organisers,' Heron ordered with a flick of his hand. 'And tell Mohammed Ali Luqman that I, personally, will wring his bloody neck if there's even a whiff of trouble.'

Freeman rocked off the desk on to his feet. 'Right you are, sir.' Cooper was already at the door and Freeman made to follow him, but then he stopped for a moment and turned back to Heron. 'Oh. Incidentally, old boy, how's Ciss? And, er, Mrs Heron?'

Heron winced. 'All right,' he said. 'Bit tired.'

Freeman tapped his finger to his forehead in casual respect and left.

Heron now thought of Pamela as he'd left her that morning, and as she'd been last night when he'd sat down on their bed: her back to him, her yellow hair matted and uncurled, her cotton nightie unwashed. She was so still in her long sleeps these days it frightened him.

He thought of how he'd tentatively reached out for her flesh and found it clammy, cool; how for that moment his heart had pumped noisily. But she'd wordlessly shrugged him off and pulled herself deeper into the sheets.

He'd stood over her in his starched police uniform, his socks pulled high, his laces tied, not knowing whether to try to kiss her shoulder; whether to tell her he was sorry, that he was worried; whether to call Dr Christie. No, not that, he decided. She wouldn't want Dr Christie.

If she was even aware of him watching over her, she didn't show it.

And there, he supposed, she still lay.

Certainly not 'all right'.

He leant quickly across his desk for the phone. But it sat next to an official portrait of the King, framed in leather, and at the sight of this he hesitated. Then he lifted the receiver and dialled Malcolm Ingram, the Police Commissioner.

BERNARD SWEET

Strange Encounter

AFTER THE EVENTS of the morning, all I wanted was to sit somewhere quiet and contemplate the world without the world contemplating me. I made my way down to the sea-front and looked out at the ruffled grey ocean. The beach was deserted and the low clouds reflected back the mournful cry of the seagulls. Much as I preferred my own company I knew that I needed to be among people, to feel the rub of humanity dispel my feelings of loneliness and dread. Just so long as they didn't come too close.

You may think it strange that someone of my evident good taste and fondness for the finer things in life should head for a chain-store café but it was one of my favourite places to go people-watching. I could remember when such establishments had proudly been labelled 'cafeterias'. Now they had pretensions of grandeur, preferring to be called 'restaurants' but it made no difference to the eating experience. You grabbed a tray and shuffled along looking at an assortment of unappealing dishes that were slowly drying out under an array of heat-lamps.

As I ambled in, the lovely but well-upholstered Madge detected my presence from behind the counter and homed in on me like a school matron scenting puberty, 'Can I tempt you with a bacon roll?' Her eyes widened suggestively as her tongue relished the words, 'and how about a little sauce?'

I looked down at the shrivelled rashers that were curling up with embarrassment and felt the cholesterol thicken in my veins. The chips would have leered at me but were too tired to make the effort and the eggs were developing the kind of wrinkled skin normally seen on the faces of fading soap stars who have spent too much time 'resting' in Ibiza.

'Not today, my angel. No, today you will fulfil my desires if you could just provide me with a pot of tea and a packet of biscuits.'

Our eyes met and I could see Madge considering a myriad other ways she could satisfy my desires, 'So it's just tea, then,' she said flatly.

'That and the warmth of your love will set my heart aglow.'

Madge busied herself with the task of funnelling hot water in the right direction then made great play of slowly and suggestively cleaning the steam spout.

She plonked the teapot, cup and saucer on my tray, 'You help yourself to the biscuits, and you know what else you can help yourself to any time.' She gave me a huge wink and I selected a pack of shortcake biscuits and beat a hasty retreat before my nerve broke.

Fully equipped, I meandered into the seating area and looked around at the other diners – a couple of tourists driven inside by the gloomy weather, a group of schoolkids reluctant to make their way to the claustrophobia of a crowded home, and a sprinkling of old age pensioners reminding themselves that they weren't on their own. I was glad to note that there were enough people to give some sense of life but plenty of room to find a table all to myself.

I just wanted to sit and lick my wounds and work out my next move. I lowered myself into a chair and regarded the tray. A pool of water had spilt on one side where the teapot had been over-filled. I hastily retrieved my biscuits, worried that I might suffer from premature dunkulation. The spoon clattered to the floor and with a weary sigh I bent down to retrieve it. It was as I groped around the floor that I became aware of the presence. My fingers had just curled round the spoon when I felt something loom, and then I saw the feet. They were encased in a pair of thick-soled black leather shoes. The shoes were unadorned and were they not emerging from a pair of grey serge trousers might have been taken to be working boots. There was something about the toecaps that suggested a steel lining. I retrieved the spoon and slowly righted myself.

The image that confronted me could have been a still from a Humphrey Bogart movie. The character sitting opposite wore a grey fedora hat pulled forward to shade his face and a tightly belted trench coat. I glanced around the restaurant but there were still plenty of spare seats and plenty of spare tables, so there was no call for this kind of unwarranted intimacy.

I contemplated moving, but even as I did so I knew that the timing was wrong. The stranger had taken advantage of my distraction and there was no escape. I was never one to shrink from eye contact and in a last bid to scare off this interloper I stared directly at him. He stared back. There was no aggression but in answer to my challenge he merely took off his hat and placed it on the table as though to claim possession. Clearly I was up against a professional.

The removal of the hat ruined the illusion. The face that was revealed was not the lean, tough one of Bogart but was round and somewhat bloated. The trespasser was not that dissimilar to me in build and complexion. True, he was dark-haired and seemed to have an addiction to Brylcreem, but the face beneath the slicked-back hair was florid and moon-shaped and although the shoulders were broad the impression was one of heaviness rather than fitness. The man's eyes were not particularly large and their colour was hard to describe, although the pupils struck me as unusually black. The nose was as florid as the cheeks and a moustache nestled between it and the slightly damp upper lip. It struck me that in other circumstances this character could have been someone's beneficent uncle or the landlord of a medieval hostelry, but the blankness of the eyes told another story. This man could be a civil servant, but not one ensconced behind a Whitehall desk; no, this one would be at home in the Third Reich. He was the sort that coolly devised the final solution, not out of hatred or vindictiveness, but because it was a job to be done, a problem to be solved. The phrase 'the banality of evil' drifted into my mind and the vague anxiety I had been feeling suddenly congealed into the fear that I might not make it out of the restaurant alive.

Having tried the stare and failed miserably, I settled down to studiously ignoring my companion. This might have worked had the stranger not reached forward and with great deliberation taken one of the biscuits out of the packet that lay open on my tray. He dunked it in his tea and then with practised efficiency transferred it to his mouth. My eyes followed the trajectory of his hand in silent disbelief. I heard a smack of the lips and couldn't help noticing the residue of wet crumbs that now decorated his moustache. The stranger did not acknowledge the theft as he reached forward and lifted his cup to his mouth. He made a slight but discernible slurp and returned the cup to the table. I noticed that he had no teapot, just a cup and saucer with a shape very different from mine. My cup had some vague pretension to style. It was plain white but shaped like a bowl so that as I drank I was presented with a pleasantly wide opening. The stranger's cup was made of thick, cream-coloured porcelain and had straight sides, more like a small mug. It was almost as though we were drinking in different establishments, even different eras. His cup had the effect of taking me back to my youth, when tea was the only hot drink you could find on the high street, and it was served in porcelain so thick it might have been used as sanitary ware.

Once again the hand reached forward and casually appropriated one of the biscuits. It was intolerable, yet somehow I felt unable to protest. Some sense of ownership had to be asserted, so I slowly reached forward and claimed a biscuit for myself. Our eyes locked but again all I saw was blankness. There were six biscuits in the packet and slowly the two of us worked our way through them, taking it in turns to claim our prize. As this curious exchange unfolded I made another intriguing observation. Each mouthful of biscuit was accompanied by a sip of tea, yet as the last piece of biscuit disappeared between the man's lips and he took another slurp of tea, I realised, as the cup returned to the table, that it was still full.

This simple fact made a deep impression on me and it was as I was considering its implications that my companion spoke, 'Go and fetch some more biscuits, will you?'

I took a deep breath to give a suitably robust response, but instead was amazed to find myself standing at the till paying for another packet of biscuits with Madge's voracious eyes hungrily staring at me. I could not remember leaving my seat and in the shock of realisation I nearly dropped my change. I whirled around and saw the hunched back of the trenchcoat.

I turned back to Madge and gestured at the table, 'Does he come here often?'

Madge winked, 'That's an old line coming from you. But just to let you know I'll come as often as you like, here or anywhere you can name.'

I blinked and tried again, 'Tell me about the guy at the table.'

Madge's breast started to heave and she leant forward and whispered huskily, 'On the table? Now you're talking!'

I shook my head, smiled politely and backed warily away. I stomped sullenly across to the table, laid the biscuits down and watched as the stubby fingers skilfully opened the packet.

Somewhere in my subconscious my 'fight or flight' response was in no doubt that the best thing I could do was leave and leave quickly. But once again there I was sitting down sharing biscuits with this worryingly odd stranger. No more words were spoken as we both engaged in this silent shortcake communion. The cup was returned to the table and I again noted that it was still full with steam drifting from its hot surface.

My self-invited guest cleared his throat, 'That was most acceptable.' Then I felt the eyes examining me. 'Your service is required. You must deal with her.'

I looked up just in time for Madge to catch my eye and wink very slowly. A cold shudder went down my spine. I looked from Madge back to the face opposite to see if there was any family resemblance. Could it be that this was some offended brother who had turned up to demand that I do the decent thing? Obviously not, the last thing on Madge's mind was anything decent.

'Deal with?' I enquired tentatively.

The phrase was repeated with the weariness of a teacher leading a particularly inept pupil, 'You must deal with her.'

I thought, 'It's not Madge, it can't be. So what the hell is he going on about?' What I said was, 'I'm sorry but I think you've got the wrong man.'

The heavy frame leant forward and the small eyes seemed to loom large. They really were a very deep black. I felt as though someone was sifting through my life like a dealer at a car boot sale. Most things were being dismissed as worthless but apparently there were one or two items 'of interest'.

The voice came again, somewhere between a whisper and a growl, 'Have you not felt her eye upon you? Is not Death already stalking you?'

Now I was truly terrified. That voice bypassed my ears and reverberated in the fear centres of my brain. The panic that had been gestating in my stomach now spread throughout my body, paralysing my limbs. The images that flashed in front of my eyes had nothing to do with Madge and everything to do with visions of death and destruction. I saw a burning flame that never quenched, I saw the sun eclipsed by the wings of a giant bat, I saw large reptilian eyes that glowered with hatred, I saw a table laden with opulent chinaware and a rather nice set of silver cutlery. Finally I saw a solitary figure in a fedora hat and a trenchcoat sitting at a table drinking an endless cup of tea whilst all around him the world ignited.

'But what's this got to do with . . .'

As I said the words the lights began to flicker. There was a loud bang and then darkness. I heard various voices raised in consternation but then the lights came on again and the commotion relaxed into nervous laughter. The only one not laughing was me. The chair opposite was empty . . .

CELIA REYNOLDS
Swan Song

'TONIGHT, Eloise, star attraction of Petrov's Circus of the Spectacular, will give her final performance on the solo trapeze . . .' The rumour, first uttered by the loose-lipped contortionist from Bow, began as little more than a low rumble, almost imperceptible at first. But it had gathered momentum with disarming alacrity, spreading to the four winds like mercury slipping through fingers powerless to contain it. 'Why now,' her fellow performers speculated, 'at the height of her career?' It did not seem possible. She was barely twenty-three.

While the mood of the performers and roustabouts alike was one of sombre incredulity, it remained, none the less, the blistering height of summer, and the two shows scheduled to take place that day were already sold out. August was a time of long-awaited holidays, Rocket ice lollies and flake-topped cones, and in this latest seaside town – whose name many of the crew could barely even recall, so marked was its similarity to the countless seaside towns that had preceded it – the tourist season was at its peak. A sliver of sea air sporadically wafted over the Big Top whenever the breeze could rouse itself to blow, and a cloying heat clung like treacle to the roustabouts' skin, leaving in its wake a sticky sea-salt veneer, the remnants of a hurried dip taken earlier that afternoon. As they sat on the promenade wolfing down crusty rolls and cold beer, even the usually ebullient seagulls appeared giddy along the shore.

The matinée had pulsed with a vibrant human current and now, as the punters arrived for the evening performance, the warm night air filled with a pungent medley of Lucky Luke's Fish'n'Chips, burnt sugar from the toffee apple-stand, and frying fat belched unapologetically into the ether from the thriving hot-dog van. Artemis Blunt, Petrov's technical supervisor for over thirty years, sensed a nervousness in the air such as he hadn't experienced since the previous summer, when Hatchet the Clown had burst into the ring with a loaded gun in the pocket of his oversized pantaloons. As the performers relaxed backstage, smoking, and drinking strong Polish coffee, Hatchet had caught his wife, Rosalie, pressed up against one of the horse trucks in a knee trembler with a temporary ring worker. Inconsolable – but determined none the less that the show must go on – he had downed half a bottle of whisky and filched an animal tranquiliser gun before staggering, blind with anger, into the ring. The euphoric crowd, completely ignorant of his distress, thought it was all part of the act. They couldn't have known that the swaying, erratic gait and the tears pouring down Hatchet's face were real, not the result of a carefully disguised water prop. Mercifully, the day had been saved by Whoop and Wallop, the rookie – or 'First of May' in circus parlance – clown act from Bruges. In an inspired moment of improvisation, they unicycled their way into the ring behind Hatchet, dismounted, and tossed a large hessian sack over his head. The mock kidnap bid proceeded with Whoop and Wallop wheeling Hatchet away in a trolley painted like a fire engine, with much tooting of horns on their part, and vehement protestations from Hatchet who struggled helplessly to reach for the gun, much to the hilarity of the crowd.

But tonight was different.

Artemis, a short, wiry whippet of a man, ran a hand through his slicked-back hair and wiped an obstinate rivulet of sweat from his brow. How many times had he raced through Clown Alley, stumbling over the Joeys' props? The Joeys – the name the roustabouts gave 'clowns' – used the narrow holding area outside the back of the Big Top to store their equipment and fire themselves up before their performance. But, this evening, Artemis was in no mood for an argument with a bucket of confetti or a collapsing chair. He picked his way carefully through the veritable obstacle course of props and, having for once negotiated the route without incident, entered the back of the tent. Inside, the atmosphere was electric. The Bulgarian tumblers were just coming to the end of their act, the audience whipped into a frenzy by their gymnastic feats of sky-bound daring. Presiding over it all from his usual spot, white-gloved hands clasped tightly behind his back, was Nikolay Fedorov, Petrov's charismatic ringmaster, fifty-eight years old, with a shock of red hair barely contained beneath an imposing top hat. Artemis watched Nikolay turn to the trombone player standing behind him and enquire with his customary aplomb, 'Can someone tell me where she is? She's on in five minutes. She should be here by now.'

Artemis knew then that Nikolay had not heard the rumour. Artemis himself prayed it wasn't true: Eloise's fusion of passion, skill and daring elevated the circus's immersive power to ever-dizzying heights. For Nikolay, the man who prided himself on knowing everything about the circus, losing his star act would be devastating. And yet this bombshell had evidently eluded him. His relaxed demeanour confirmed it.

Before anyone had time to respond, the ruched velvet curtains that separated the ring from the performers' quarters swung open with a flourish, and a petite elfin figure, wrapped in a diaphanous cloak of woodland green, appeared in the shadows. Nikolay surveyed the woman's costume with a hint of surprise. 'Eloise, you are wearing green? You know some people say it should never be worn under the Big Top.'

Artemis shook his head. It was a well-known tenet of circus folklore that green was the colour of nature and a harbinger of spring, but it was a shade that quickly faded in the autumn and winter. For many circus performers, it symbolised death . . .

'I am not "some people", Kolya,' replied Eloise, enigmatic as ever. She brushed a stray lock of cropped brown hair from her face. 'Don't be so superstitious. It will light beautifully, you'll see.'

Nikolay tipped his hat with a touch of gentlemanly Victoriana as she passed by. 'Good luck, detka. We have a packed house. Be sure and give them a good show.'

Eloise nodded. 'Thank you, Kolya. Of course. I will do my best.'

The plaintive strains of a haunting melody echoed through the Big Top as the lights dimmed, and Eloise entered into the centre of the ring, illuminated by a single spotlight. A solitary rope hung from the infinite void above, its bound end skimming the powdery sawdust at her feet.

An invitation.

Eloise opened her cloak and let it fall, soft as gossamer, to the ground, and wrapped her tiny hand through the loop in the rope that would lift her high, high above the ring to the solo trapeze waiting still and expectant above.

*

Five rows back from the front of the ring, a ten-year-old girl sat rigid with anticipation. Her right hand was clasped tightly around a shiny, curved metal object; her left rested in the hand of the elderly woman sitting next to her. When Eloise entered the ring, Eirwen Evans gave her grandmother's hand a gentle squeeze and whispered, 'Nan, there she is! Isn't she beautiful?'

Eirwen had seen the show twice already, and had cajoled her grandmother into taking her one last time before the circus left town the next morning. Some hours earlier, Eirwen and her older sister Angela had wandered casually around the circus's fenced perimeter before stopping to watch the backstage preparations unfold. It was like hovering on the precipice of a mysterious, fantastical world. A curious muddle of unfamiliar music and gentle laughter filtered through the open window of a nearby trailer; a motley group of bright-eyed circus children, one of whom was dressed in a ragged harlequin costume, were chasing each other around an overturned barrel, water gushing on to the surrounding grass. Elsewhere, a bare-chested animal handler, his arms covered with intricate tattoos of climbing ivy, walked two elegant white horses around an open-air enclosure, while a bearded knife-thrower sat on an upturned wooden crate, polishing his set of knives in the sun. Their youthful strength was thrown into stark relief by the arrival of a wizened old man who set about teaching a small dog to jump through a multi-coloured hoop.

And appearing like an angel through the midst of this extraordinary and exotic landscape came Eloise, a small silver headpiece dangling from her hand. Eirwen gasped so loudly, she had to put her palm to her mouth to stop herself from crying out loud. Eloise turned to look in their direction and, after a moment's deliberation, began to weave her way towards them.

'Look!' Eirwen murmured under her breath to her sister, 'She's coming over!'

A few moments later, Eloise was standing facing the two girls on the other side of the barrier. 'Hello,' she said, smiling at Eirwen, 'I'm Eloise. Would you like this crown? I was taking it to the wardrobe trailer to be mended, but on second thoughts, it's not so badly damaged. And besides,' she added after a beat, 'I won't be needing it any more.' She slipped the delicate headpiece through one of the diamond-shaped holes in the fence and dropped it into Eirwen's outstretched hand.

Angela nudged her sister in the ribs. 'Well, what do you say?'

Eirwen adjusted the candy-floss-coloured glasses on the bridge of her nose and looked at Eloise in amazement. 'Can I have it? Really? Won't you need it for your performance?'

'No,' Eloise replied, 'Think of it as a little memento. This evening I will perform without it. And after tonight, who knows when I may fly again?' With that she turned and disappeared once more amongst the sprawling jumble of trailers behind her.

Eirwen stood gazing in awe at her prize, Eloise's words still hanging prophetically in the air.

*

The contortionist Rosalie Hatchet was pegging her husband's stage clothes on to a makeshift washing line strung between two adjacent trailers when Eloise walked back from the perimeter fence, her head bowed. Rosalie stopped what she was doing and stood perfectly still, hidden by the prodigious mass of her husband's pantaloons. She was certain Eloise had not seen her and could scarcely believe what she had just heard. How long had she had to demean herself by playing second fiddle to that so-called 'Queen of the solo trapeze', while she, Rosalie, was relegated further and further down the bill?

Sidling casually towards her neighbour's open door, she let the words spew forth from her mouth like a contagion. 'Our French ingénue has finally lost her nerve. I just heard Eloise say she takes her final bow tonight. I bet that over-possessive father has caught up with her at last.'

Her neighbour's eyebrows arched.

The contagion, liberated from its host, slowly began to spread.

*

Agota, the Hungarian tight-rope walker, was playing cards with her brother Andras in their gaudily painted trailer when Eloise appeared unannounced, looking somewhat troubled, at their door.

'What's wrong?' Agota asked with a wink, 'Has that Hatchet woman been sticking pins in your effigy again?'

Eloise shook her head and indicated with a discreet movement of her eyes that she wished to speak with Agota alone. Andras looked from one to the other, shrugged, slipped a half-smoked packet of cigarettes into his pocket and obligingly stepped outside. Agota closed the door behind him and motioned to Eloise to sit down.

'I saw him, Agi,' Eloise began, 'Last night I saw him watching the encampment from the promenade. I never thought I'd see him again. I begged him to go back to France and forget me. I told him my life is here now, that it's too late to go back to the way things were. But it was a lie.'

'Eloise, it's never too late,' said Agota, rising. 'When did you last speak with him?'

'Two, maybe three weeks ago. He's been following the circus ever since he came here in June. And there's something else. Today I found out – '

'Hello? Is anyone in there?' Their conversation was interrupted by three loud knocks on the trailer door. It was Artemis, clipboard under his arm, a large mug of tea in his hand. 'Let's go, girls, the boss wants to see everyone in the ring right away. One of his pep talks, you know the drill. Tonight is the last show before we hit the road again and it looks like we're going to do record business, so he wants to make sure everyone's on top of their game.'

Agota and Eloise had no choice but to follow Artemis and join the rest of the troupe in the Big Top. Agota wondered what her friend had wanted to say, but Nikolay kept everyone rounded up, tetchy and skittish as wild horses, for so long that there was no opportunity for them to talk alone again that day.

*

Unaware of the rumour spreading through the ranks, Eloise hurried back to her trailer before the evening curtain call was announced and wrote a note to Agota, and a second to Nikolay. Ending each one with the salutation, 'Take care, my dear friend. See you down the road,' she sealed both envelopes and left them where they would find them the following morning. The letters would tell them everything they needed to know. She owed them that much, at least.

Eloise pulled on her costume, cast a lingering glance at the transformation staring back at her in the mirror, then crossed herself and switched off the light.

Showtime.

*

Suspended high up in the air, Eloise sits poised on her solo trapeze. With effortless grace, she extends her legs and propels the trapeze forwards, then bends her knees, folds her legs under and swings backwards, repeating the sequence over and over, all the while gathering speed.

Her birdlike frame is enveloped in a bodysuit of palest green and, with each tumble and turn, the intricate beadwork catches the light, leaving a kaleiodoscopic trail of colour through the air. There is no safety net below, only a discreet harness keeps her from harm, one end attached by a metal clip to her waist, the other disappearing into the blackness above.

She inhales deeply.

Inside the Big Top, everything is still except for the shimmering spotlight that tick-tocks back and forth, pursuing her every move like a kitten chasing a shadow on a summer's day.

An eclectic group of fellow artistes gather backstage to watch her fly. Rosalie sits apart from the rest, a cigarette dangling from scarlet lips, her heavy stage make-up giving off a ghoulish glow in the semi-darkness. No one dares look Nikolay in the eye. Focused and alert as always, the supreme showman stands with feet firmly planted, cane in hand, calmly looking on.

As the breathtaking majesty of Eloise's act unfolds, Rosalie looks away with undisguised disdain. She has never been able to move audiences in that way. 'Transcendent,' the critics called Eloise on her solo trapeze, 'Otherworldly,' 'Utterly sublime,' while Rosalie's own performance was once referred to as a 'Freakish novelty act of contorted limbs, occasionally too unbearable to behold.'

The crowd below stares, mesmerised by the fearless creature above, yet Eloise's expression remains impassive, her face a sea of magenta and forest green, the colours of a Faerie Queen.

She exhales.

Maciej, the Polish fire-eater, turns to Andras and says, 'Look at her fly! She is magnificent!'

Eloise's rhythmic breath continues.

Her acrobatics become more daring, now hanging upside down, now standing astride the trapeze; the crowd sees only the manifestations of its own dreams and fears. And then! the Faerie Queen slips. It happens so quickly it's impossible to know if it's part of the act, but as the crowd gasps in awe Eloise catches herself at the last moment, looping her left knee over the bar and dangling upside down, limp and languid as a dying swan, before righting herself once again to spontaneous, rapturous applause.

Eloise gazes into the darkness ahead. She doesn't see Eirwen gripping her silver crown, transfixed, her heart beating so fast she feels as though it might burst from her chest; she doesn't see Nikolay standing in the wings, a mixture of professional pride and genuine wonder on his age-worn face; she doesn't see any of the troupe, or the band, or the adoring crowd at her feet.

And yet she instinctively knows that in the shadows below, the young man has come to watch her one more time. He is the childhood sweetheart her father forbade her to see. The small town boy he said would ruin his daughter's career because he had no talent of his own other than to make her happy. Arrived from France just two months earlier, he had finally mustered the courage to seek her affections once more. He is Benoit Moget, the man Eloise loved from the moment they first met, sitting next to each other at a provincial circus show a decade before.

She senses him now, standing there with his tousled curls and the pale, angular face that reflects the light as he gazes overhead. She can hear the urgency of his words, still: 'Up there, when you fly, you brush against the stars and caress the moon. It's where you belong, Eloise! All I ask is that you let me be here for you when you come back to earth.'

As the music reaches its climax, Benoit watches patiently and waits. In the pocket of his jeans his hand curls gently around a small antique box, a box containing a ring.

Above him, high above them all, lost in the purity of the moment, Eloise closes and opens her eyes wide in a moment of perfect clarity. As her performance draws to a close, she focuses only on her breath, with its steady inhale, exhale, inhale, exhale, and the imperceptible but none the less vital heartbeat of the baby growing in her womb, stretched flat and taut across the bar.

AMANDA SAINT

As if I Were a River

1

T HE HEAT from the radiator starts to burn my legs through my skirt as I watch the road through the rain streaming down the window. Where has he got to? Although I always worry whenever he's late home or meeting me somewhere, I never tell him about my fears. I know he'll call them irrational. I just can't seem to help it though. Even when everything seems like it's going along just fine, underneath there's always that fear that things will change suddenly, without warning, and there will be absolutely nothing I can do about it – after all, they have before. Through the blur of rain I see something move up near the corner. At last, Jimmy! But no. It's a plastic bag dancing in the wind. When he still doesn't come round the corner I go into the kitchen. It's like going to the toilet in a restaurant when you're waiting for your food and hoping that it will turn up while you're gone. Maybe if I stop staring out the window he'll come through the front door. So I go and sit down at the kitchen table and wait. And wait. And wait. The hands on the clock above the cooker don't seem to move, unlike mine as my fingers drum and fidget on the table. Another forty-five minutes pass. I feel sick, shaky but strangely removed. Like I'm watching myself wait.

'Nothing's wrong. He'll be back in a minute, of course he will,' I say out loud.

The sound of my voice in the silent kitchen unnerves me, spurs me into action. I pick up Jimmy's mobile from the top of the fridge where he's left it, as if by doing so I can somehow magic him back into contact, and then slam it straight back down again in frustration at not knowing what to do. Why does he always leave it behind? Another ten minutes pass.

I have to go and look for him. I grab my coat from the hook in the hallway, stuffing my keys and phone in the pocket as I shrug it on. The wind blows the front door out of my hand as I open it and flings stinging needles of rain in my face.

Apart from a lone fox walking away from me in the middle of the road, his fur glowing orange in the streetlights, everywhere is deserted. Have you seen him? I want to ask. I like the foxes, always feel a sense of wonder when I come across one. Jimmy says that's one of the things he loves about me – my love of the animal world, which sees me rescuing baby birds that have fallen out of their nests and even a duck once when we were walking by the river. Somehow it had got stuck on its back with its legs in the air so I'd picked it up and put it back on its webbed feet. It had felt so soft, I'd wanted to bury my face in it.

A gust of wind gets me moving and I turn left to go next-door first. I need to tell someone what's happening. Maybe it will get rid of the weird detachment I'm feeling if I say it out loud. I ring Gloria's bell and hope that she's not out, or in bed. The intercom buzzes and then her voice says hello with a note of concern evident in it.

'Glor, it's Kate. Jimmy's gone out and not come back. I'm really worried,' I blurt out.

Gloria, well used to my worrying, sighs and the door release buzzes. 'Oh Kate, come on in then.'

When she opens the door into her flat she's in her pyjamas and an aroma of recently devoured pizza lingers around her. I can tell she's feeling weary of me and my constant fretting over terrible scenarios that only happen in my head. Gloria moved in the same weekend Jimmy and I did, nine months or so ago, and we'd chatted as we carried our worldly possessions up the parallel steps leading to our flats. Then we became friends. She moved here after being in a women's refuge, hiding from a crazy boyfriend who had beaten her so badly and so often that she nearly ended up dead. It took that near-death experience to finally get her to leave him. Jimmy and I moved here from Hammersmith as it's cheaper and we're saving to buy our own place one day.

'So, tell me then,' Gloria says as she walks away from me down the hallway to the kitchen.

'I know I worry all the time but this time I really think something's wrong.'

There's a panicky edge in my voice and Gloria must have heard it too as she looks quite worried. But she holds up the kettle to see if I just want tea and reassurance as usual. I shake my head.

'We've been out for dinner and when we got back Jimmy said he'd run out of cigarettes so he went to the shop and he hasn't come back and he's been gone well over an hour and he's left his phone behind. I've got to go and look for him.'

In my panic, my words are tumbling over each other like the leaves outside in the wind.

'Maybe he's bumped into someone he knows and stopped to have a chat, or gone for a pint with them,' Gloria reasons, 'or the shop was shut and he had to go to a different one.'

'No. The pubs are all shut by now and Eddie's shop never shuts at this time. Something's happened.'

I know I sound crazy but the shop's only a five minute walk away, he should have been back ages ago and I've got a terrible feeling. More than I've ever had before. Gloria nods as if she agrees with me but I know she just wishes I'd calm down, maybe even that she hadn't answered the door. She gives a loud, exaggerated sigh.

'Do you want me to come down to the shops with you?'

I nod.

*

As we approach the row of shops, the two boys who are almost always hanging around outside are in their usual spot. This time, though, they are not alone. They've got a small tan puppy with them that looks like it's only a couple of months old. Gloria looks nervous; these boys probably remind her of the crazy boyfriend she's hiding from. I would never normally have made friends with someone like Gloria, but the moving-in day broke the ice between us and despite our differences we just clicked. We must look like an odd couple though, battling through the wind and rain, her in a cheap nylon hooded coat, tracksuit bottoms and trainers, me in my top-to-toe black tailoring because I went straight from work to meet Jimmy earlier. Not that I'm always so smart, but we had an important meeting with some potential advertisers today, so I dressed the part of Managing Editor for once. The boys make us both uneasy and we look down at the ground as we cover the final few meters to the shop. As we draw level with them though, I pluck up the courage to ask them whether they've seen Jimmy.

'The bloke you is always with, yeah?' the one holding the puppy's lead asks. The puppy, excited by new arrivals, jumps up against Gloria's legs.

It makes me nervous to think that they've noticed us before. But I'm being stupid. Why wouldn't they have noticed us? We've seen them nearly every day since we moved in, and we've noticed them. I nod in answer to his question and quickly meet his eyes before looking back down at my shoes again. Up close he's got acne scars all over his face, glaring red.

'Nah, we ain't seen him, 'ave we Jinks. Not today anyway.'

Jinks shakes his head slowly just once before staring off into the distance again with a look of complete indifference.

'Why, lost him 'ave ya?' Acne-face laughs.

I nod and shake my head in confusion as I turn quickly away to go into the shop, Gloria close behind me. The heat and the noise from the TV both hit me with equal force as I push the door open. The sound of motor racing drones around the shop, the excited shouting of the commentator bouncing off the tins of baked beans and cans of Strongbow cider. My eyes instantly dry out as there isn't a drop of moisture left in the air. Eddie, who came to London from the Philippines just last year, has got several blow heaters going in an attempt to keep out the English cold. Even in the summer he'd had at least one going most of the time. He looks up at us from his seat behind the counter, tearing his eyes from the TV which is perched on a three-legged wooden stool just a couple of feet in front of him.

'Hello,' he says with a smile as he recognises us both.

'Hi Eddie,' I say as I try to smile at him. It feels more like a grimace though, and Eddie's own smile falters before dropping off his face completely as he asks if something is wrong. My mouth is suddenly as dry as my eyes and I can't answer so Gloria tells him we're looking for Jimmy.

'Ah, your lovely young man,' he nods his head towards me. 'No, I haven't seen him today.'

As this sinks in I suddenly find my voice again. 'Are you sure? He left home about an hour ago to come down here and get some cigarettes.'

Eddie shakes his head slowly. A piece of his hair escapes from whatever it is he slicks it back with and falls down over his eyes. He pushes it back unconsciously as he repeats that he hasn't seen him. Gloria thanks him then takes my arm and leads me gently away. I can see the confusion I'm feeling mirrored in her face as we both wonder what on earth is going on. On the pavement outside the shop we both stand, stunned, for a second, trying to make sense of what we've just learnt. Jimmy hasn't been in the shop. Gloria recovers first and links her arm through mine.

'Come on Kate, let's go home. I bet he's there now and is wondering where you've got to.'

I know this isn't true though as if he was he'd be ringing my phone to find out where I'd gone. The boys are sitting at the bus stop opposite the shop.

'Maybe he's doing the dirty on ya. Shacked up with someone else,' Acne-face calls across the road. Both boys find this hilarious and as Gloria and I hurry off they slap each other on the back and laugh as if they had just discovered they are the most talented comedians in the country.

'Ignore them, Kate. Stupid boys.' Gloria pulls me tighter to her as we round the corner to our street.

As we get closer to our flats I can see Cheddar waiting on the doorstep to be let in. Much as I love Cheddar, my heart sinks when I see him.

'Jimmy's not back then or he would have let Cheddar in.'

Gloria looks up at Cheddar. 'I bet he's indoors.'

I shake my head. Somehow I just know that he isn't.

We walk up the steps and I can sense the emptiness of the flat before we go in. From the hallway you can see into the kitchen and living room. Empty. The doors to the bathroom and bedrooms are closed.

'Jimmy?' Gloria calls.

Silence.

She tries again. Nothing.

We walk to the kitchen and sit down at the table.

'He must have seen someone he knows,' says Gloria.

'But who? None of his friends live round here. And where would they have gone? He was tired, it's late he wouldn't have just gone out with someone.'

Gloria doesn't respond but gets up and puts the kettle on.

'There'll be a simple explanation, you'll see.' She says as she gets the cups out of the dishwasher. 'He'll be back any minute now.'

By the time we've drunk our tea there is still no sign of Jimmy. I return to my post at the front window and look down the street. Deserted still.

'It's been almost two hours now, Glor.'

'Maybe we should ring the police.'

'The police? I don't think they'll do anything till someone's been missing at least twenty-four hours.'

'Maybe something has happened. Did you see the news earlier? There's riots in town. Students.'

'Riots? What's that got to do with anything?'

'I don't know. Nothing. But you never know who he could have seen out there.'

'Don't say that.'

We stare at each other in silence, neither of us knowing what to do next. The hands on the clock above the cooker seem to be whirring round now and before we know it, it's almost 3 a.m. and Jimmy still hasn't come back.

'Ring the hospitals, Kate. Maybe he's had an accident.' Gloria chews on her thumbnail as she says this. She seems almost as worried as I am. So I call St Thomas's and St George's A&E departments but they haven't had anyone admitted under Jimmy's name.

I put down the phone. 'There's nothing we can do now, Glor. Let's go to bed. Go home and I'll see you tomorrow. Today, I mean.'

'Are you sure? I can stay if you want.'

'No, it's okay. I'll be okay.'

I go and lie down on the bed, knowing that I won't sleep. But if I don't at least pretend to go to bed then Gloria won't go home. And I really want her to. I just want to be on my own, but she hovers in the bedroom doorway.

'Ring me if he comes back. When he comes back.'

I nod and she finally leaves.

As soon as I hear the front door shut behind her I get back up and go into the kitchen again. Cheddar is sleeping on his favourite chair next to the radiator and I pick him up and rub my cheek on his face. He purrs. He's such a big softy, Cheddar, despite his butch ginger tom appearance. Jimmy has been gone for over four hours. I put Cheddar back on his chair and pick up Jimmy's mobile again from the top of the fridge and scroll through his recent calls and texts to see if there's anything out of the ordinary. Just me, Alan, Baz, Martin. The usual suspects. Then it occurs to me that he could have been deleting things he doesn't want me to see. I laugh out loud at that, it just seems completely unfeasible, but it's a brittle laugh that's going to splinter any moment and it scares me so I stop.

The cat flap bursts open as Cheese, Cheddar's sister, comes hurtling in. I jump and put Jimmy's phone down quickly on the kitchen table as if I shouldn't be looking at it. Cheese does a quick turn round each of my legs, rubs her face briefly on my left shin and then joins Cheddar on his chair and snuggles down to sleep next to him. I don't know what to do with myself. I remember what Gloria said about the riots so switch the TV on to the 24-hour news channel. The images of students ransacking Westminster then being kettled on the bridge for hours seem even more surreal than the fact that Jimmy popped out to the shop all those hours ago and hasn't come back. It's miles away from Battersea anyway so it can't have had anything to do with Jimmy. What has happened, then? Where has he gone?

I go back into the bedroom and lie down on the bed again, thinking that I should try to sleep. I roll over on to my right side, facing the window, wrapping myself in the duvet as I go. The curtains are open and the rain is still falling, the wind still throwing it around. Cheddar comes padding into the room and jumps up onto the bed. He circles twice and then curls up by my feet and goes back to sleep. He likes to always be in the same room with me. Even the bathroom – he sits and watches when I shower and dips his feet in when I have a bath.

When we'd got Cheddar and Cheese as kittens, I hadn't been convinced – I've always been more of a dog person, but Jimmy has always had cats and he went on and on for ages until I gave in. He was so excited when he brought them home and as soon as I saw them sitting in the carry box with their big blue eyes and ears that were too big for their dinky little heads I was completely won over. We'd sat on the sofa with one each on our laps, Cheddar for me and Cheese for Jimmy. Names that Jimmy insisted on and thinks are hilarious but I just find a bit embarrassing. Whenever I have to call them in from outside I just shake the food box and call out 'Pussy cats' as I can't bring myself to shout their names in case the neighbours hear me. We'd just watched them sleep for ages, grinning stupidly at each other every now and then. I hug his pillow and try to swallow the panic that's bubbling up inside me.

My phone starts ringing in the kitchen where I left it. I jump out of bed and run to answer it. It's got to be Jimmy! But it rings off before I can get to it and the number has been withheld. Oh Jimmy, where are you? Was that you? If not, who was it?

KEVIN FRANKE

The Order of Things

THEY BROUGHT ME HERE after I used the cheese grater to grind through my knuckles. My skin came off just like parmesan, in fleshy little flakes. There isn't much skin on your knuckles and you hit the bone pretty quickly.

Patient 2108JX
Patient lost consciousness after scraping off superficial layer of bone with a kitchen grating device during severe psychotic episode. Admitted and sectioned under Mental Health Act. Danger to herself and others. First session. Patient agitated, sweating heavily, hands trembling.

And so now I sit around and I look at the white walls and the white floor and the white ceiling. I sit here and I look at all this white all the time. White bandages on my hands. All I see is white. Nothing else: just white. It's not all the same white though, you see, do you notice that, Dr Pavani? Well, I do. I notice different whites because I'm looking at the white all day.

I want to talk about my sister. Something I want to say about my sister but I can't remember what. Definitely something though, yes. Do you know what it is?

Patient makes frequent references to her sister 'K', both to myself and clinic staff, but appears unable to recollect much detail about their relationship. Closed body language whenever talking of sister, crossed arms, crossed legs. Met with sister separately yesterday to discuss patient.

I can remember things from way back, but I struggle to remember last week. Remembering is hard for me these days. Like when you're sat on the toilet and you know you need to pee, but you're having to concentrate on peeing, and you try really hard to make yourself but you can't. That's what it's like: as if my brain's trying to piss memories but it can't.

What I do remember is buttering my toast that morning and taking a few bites and noticing that it tasted unusual. I couldn't tell what the taste was, so I took a few more bites, always from around the edges, because I like to eat my toast all around the edges first and work my way towards the middle. Then it occurred to me what it was. My butter tasted of hate. Hate, yes. That was it. I knew there was something odd about it. I'm convinced they knew exactly what they were selling me at the shop, trying to sell it to me as normal butter when really it was contaminated. Knowingly selling me this hate-spread! I could tell by the way the cashier looked at me that he was a crook. So there I was, sat at the kitchen table, staring at this hated toast in front of me. I wanted to know what it would feel like on my skin. I took off my dress and bra and pants and I worked the knob of hate-butter into my skin, smearing it all over myself. It felt amazing, warming and nourishing, and it made my skin feel so soft. It was exactly what I needed. I needed to feel something again, something real and precise, if only for a minute: to feel pure hate on my skin like that. I enjoyed it.

Notes from patient's GP records refer to an increasing obsession with the word 'hate', dating back to March 2011. Patient appears to think of it as a virus-like substance, something that can be caught and passed on. Records note recurring severe eczema on hands from obsessive hand-washing. Ward staff have observed continuing compulsive behaviour.

And then I panicked a bit, because I was completely covered in this grease and I was worried I might have some sort of adverse reaction.

Can hate seep through your skin? Does it attack your organs? I wasn't sure. I tried to google it but found nothing, so I quickly de-buttered myself using two loaves of sliced bread. That was before. Before the grater. I remember that. I remember the order of things that day.

Patient struggling to place things chronologically, experiencing disrupted sense of time. Potentially related to medication: monitor over next 30 days and then review. Reduce dose if necessary/safe. Switch medication if needed. Concerns not to be disclosed to patient at any point.

It was my father who taught me to be cautious about catching viruses and picking up bacteria. He was always washing his hands with these large chunks of vegetable soap, scrubbing away furiously. His hands were always dry and raw from all the scrubbing, covered in flaking skin. I rubbed lotion into his hands for him whilst he was napping on the sofa in front of the TV. When I saw him in the coffin at the funeral home he was turned out so well, his best suit on, hair combed perfectly, but I looked at his hands and they were dry and peeling still. I made me sad to think we were burying him with his hands like that, so I moisturised them once more whilst paying my final respects.

On that morning, before I made the toast, I'd woken up with the music again: the music inside my head. So loud. Couldn't hear myself think.

Patient showing signs of paranoia. Sister confirmed patient started to hear voices late 2011 and frequently claimed to be hearing music. Monitor patient for any further auditory hallucinations.

So the music was in my head that morning, really very loud. Hard to describe. I don't hear it much any more, not since I've been here. Anyhow. The music is like a very very angry Björk. Inside my head. Making very loud, angry Björk -music. I always did think she was a bit odd, but I didn't think her the kind of person to get quite so. Well. She does get very angry when she sings inside my head, aggressive even.

The music was there the moment I opened my eyes in the morning. I used to spend whole days with my eyes closed just because I was scared that the music would come on. I'd blind-walk through whole days, feeling my way along the walls and furniture in my flat. I had bruises all over my body the next day. But it was one way of stopping the music.

> Patient prone to aggressive outbursts. Has physically assaulted several members of staff since admittance. K also reports previous instances of lashing out, throwing of a chair, and occasional obscene verbal abuse. K often feels threatened by sister.

I am trying to become a calmer person now. That's one thing I am learning in this place. And I try to remember the order of things. I know that if I gather all the different fragments and put them back together again in the right way, then I'm okay. But I do get frightened sometimes. By the things that are happening to me. I know they're unusual and I know I'm no longer the same person as before. It's as if the person I used to be has become a shadow that's with me still, lurking, like a dark stain I notice out of the corner of my eye. I see the way people look at me. The way people look at me has changed. There is fear there, in their eyes, and also a certain repulsion. I frighten people; I can see that. Whatever has changed about me is magnified by their witnessing of it. Other people's perception of me has changed who I am.

So, I remember there was the music inside my head and I remember there was the butter. I remember those things, in that order, because that is the order they happened in. Music, then butter.

And then –

then –

music, butter – ?

Fuck –

Must remember the order –

and then I –

Then there was someone at the door. Yes, that's it. I didn't hear the doorbell because of Bjork, but I could see a shadow through the stained glass. It was a courier. A large parcel.

CAN YOU BRING IT IN FOR ME PLEASE?
(Am I shouting?)
PUT IT ON THE KITCHEN TABLE PLEASE THANK YOU.

Note: There were no deliveries that day, a Sunday. Patient presumed to have been on her own in the house for several weeks at time of sectioning. K had been on a holiday with husband and son. Signs of urination in the bedroom and signs of defecation in the hallway.

I don't know about you, but I love getting parcels. Reminds me of being a child and Christmas and birthdays and things. We used to have such lovely Christmases when I was growing up, but they were never the same again after Dad died. My mother still went through all the motions: buying presents, decorating the house and the tree, cooking turkey dinner. But then she just sat there, mute, in the big black leather armchair, staring into space, as if we weren't there at all. Didn't say a word, sometimes sat like that for days. She had nothing left to give. My sister and I used to keep whole conversations going, asking our mother questions and then assuming the answers. We had imaginary conversations with our corpse of a mother. What seasonal cheer there was we produced out of thin air. We tried hard to make things normal.

She came to visit me yesterday, my sister. We sat together and we looked at each other for a long time. We didn't speak. Just sat there, together. She held my hand, I held hers, and we looked into each other's eyes. After she left, I cried.

Conversation with patient's sister K: Confirmed she found her sister unconscious on kitchen floor, hands bleeding profusely. Bread scattered over floor, remnants of grease (butter). Called ambulance immediately.

Says they have always been close, though patient has become increasingly disturbed over previous three years. Difficult to communicate with. Relationship increasingly strained.

K found it hard to deal with patient's deterioration and was worried about consequences of seeking medical attention for her. Blames herself for severity of incident. Says mother used to show signs of depression (undiagnosed) after husband's death. Father suffered from what sounds like OCD. It was what they were used to, mother and father's behaviour never questioned or thought of as mental illness.

I knew I hadn't ordered anything, so it had to be a gift. I was really excited. I walked around the parcel a few times, inspecting it, savouring that moment before you open a present. I stood up on one of the chairs and cut through the lid with a knife. Floating inside the parcel was the Earth, as if I were watching it from space: blue, green, brown-specked, white clouds surrounding it, just like you see in those satellite photos. I removed the box and the planet just floated above the table in the middle of my kitchen. It was the most beautiful thing. I cried and cried and I understood the meaning of life. I really did. Everything suddenly made sense to me: the things that had been happening to me, and all the crazy things that were happening in the world. It was a moment of utter clarity. I felt lightheaded and I knew things were going to be okay. It was a gift from God: this floating planet in a box. He was there with me in my flat, right there, with me. I felt every cell of my body exploding, shooting outwards into space.

I climbed off the chair and I grabbed the cheese grater from the counter and started to grate through my knuckles. I wanted to grate my entire body, to sprinkle myself all over the earth, to float down on this beautiful planet like a thousand little snowflakes.

God was calling me home.

ELIZABETH BUCK

Up She Stands

U P DIANE STANDS and off she goes, stepping over reclining bodies until she reaches the kitchen door.

Reuben grunts. 'Moody cow!'

Our legs have become parallel; mine are just touching his, along the length of his outer thigh, our feet in unison, toes pointing upwards. I feel his arm moving against my shoulder as he delves his fingers into his hip pocket, reaching for his cigarette tin and his lighter. He balances the wafer paper on his hip, sprinkling it until he has a loose package of tobacco. Wriggling his hip in a snake-like movement against me, he forces a small polythene package out of his groin pocket and balances it on his thigh. He shakes the contents over the open tobacco package before twisting the paper into a tight cone and lighting it. There is a whiff of strongly scented flame and he inhales the smoke before waving his hand in front of his face and offering it to me. My instinct is to take it. As I inhale, I feel the prickling sensation of the back of his hand; he is running his knuckle against my calf and then I feel his fingers exploring under the base of my hem just below my panty line. He dampens my neck with his tongue, runs his palm over the base of my spine, loops his thumb into the crevice of my behind, gently rubbing it up and down.

His lips are now pressed against my ear. 'Let's go upstairs. I can't hear myself think in here. Just for a minute. Just for a minute.'

I slip my hand into his; we stumble up, over empty plastic cups, a brittle cascade of broken slivers into the carpet. Grasping my hand tightly in case I stumble, he guides me through the packed room to the staircase. I glance over to the front door but there's still no sign of Brian.

Looking over the banister, I can see Diane. She is standing in the kitchen, her back silhouetted against the open back door, looking out into the darkened garden. A plume of blue smoke tells me she is smoking and I see the end of the cigarette glow orange as she flicks ash into the darkness. Over her head, illuminating her like a halo, shines the perfect glacial moon, lighting her up like mercury.

Silently I am saying, 'Turn round. Turn round and see me. See me going upstairs with your boyfriend. See me and stop me now.'

But she doesn't turn. She doesn't even shift her weight; her eyes are fixed, obstinate, staring upwards; seeing nothing but the cold night air, she is refusing to be part of anything that is happening behind her.

We have reached the penultimate step. There is time; there is time for her to turn around; time for her to see us, time to catch us; but she just stands, staring up at the moon. I wonder if she is crying. I realise, of course, that this is unfair but still I am going up; up the stairs; upstairs with Reuben and going up is all that matters to me now. We cross the landing, giggling. I still have my hand in his and I am floating. We have walked over people and coats and here we are; we are cat-like in our steps and our intentions and we are invisible.

It was our priority discussion throughout our puberty: losing our virginity. When would you lose it? Would you wait until marriage? If there was a four-minute warning of nuclear attack, what would you do to ensure that you didn't die a virgin? Most of us agreed that it would be essential to lose it in the event of an impending nuclear war; we would deal with the consequences after survival, *if* there was survival. Next question was always, who with? In the event of the nuclear holocaust, precious time would be lost in finding someone of quality. Most of us agreed that it would not be Danny Bradshaw (pus-filled pimples and BO). In a fantasy situation, obviously you would be in the vicinity of Wardour Street and just walking by Keith Richards. Chances were that you would be at school; in an all-female school with only two male teachers (one fifty, one RE), it would have to be Greg the science technician. We would have to form an orderly queue and lucky Greg would have to sustain an erection at speed. Then there was opportunism: what if you were at the hairdressers? (Pansy John?) In the corner shop? (Mr Ali?) On the street on a Tuesday and it was bin day? (The young bin man with round pebble-glasses, not the older one with the beer belly?)

I lost mine during Diane's party.

When I think back, I ask myself why Brian wasn't on my nuclear list. Why did he choose to take his mum to Brighton instead of choosing to be at the party with me? Why couldn't he have the brains to see what would happen? If he had, it would *never* have happened. Well, I *say* never, but I suppose never is a long time!

The only thought that occupies me when I leave the party is what will my dad say? I walk the stretch of pavement between my house and Diane's, the strip of the shining wet metal balanced in a moonbeam and every step is ringing out to emphasise that I am on my own in this. I will never be able to tell; never be able to tell my dad; never tell Brian; definitely never tell Diane.

In the cold shine of moonlight, the alcohol is wearing off; the feeling in my face returning to normal. I feel a miserable, a demolishing sense of loss. I had expected fulfilment and passion, rushing waves, falling chimneys, but just feel grubby and foolish. It can only be me at fault, me who could be blamed. The whole combination was so wrong; too much drink, too much romantic talk, too much trust. I had never thought sex would be swift and clinical; I had imagined wooing not domination. I feel tears in my throat and struggling against sobbing anger, I attempt to turn the key in the lock of out front door. I push the key; there appears to be a disagreement between the two. I feel the key's edge, serrated and sharp, and the pattern of the keyhole, irregular and dark, but the two, although meant for each other, are incapable of linking. I stand a little way from the door, gripping the bulb of the key, and extend my arm. I close one eye to maintain a perfect aim. This creates an imbalance and the centre of my body tips over, a slow trajectory downwards

The wallflowers in the garden border come slowly and sharply into focus; I become acutely aware of their scent and my nose comes into contact with their petals before lining up with a pile of cat shit. Cold moment of truth. I am still drunk. Still pissed. Still off my face. The night air had only partially cleared my head. My face glides briefly over the flowers and my lips come into contact with the soil. Tears fall, muddy, soiled. I sob with the frustration of not being able to enter the house. I wonder how I managed to get across the road and vaguely remember not being able to open the gate, trying to proceed with dignity as I climbed over Diane's picket fence. I remember that as my foot touched the wood, the gate had swung open and the force had precipitated me on to the pavement. I glanced back. The curtains of the house remained closed; the music thumped on and no one had come after me. I had struggled to my feet, brushed my dirt-stained dress down and proceeded across the street to where I was now: face down in my own flower bed. I support myself against the wall until I am upright and at last manage to open the door.

A voice from the kitchen. 'What time do you call this?'

I make a bolt for the stairs, hammering up to the landing, leaving my pyjama-clad dad standing at the bottom, mug of cooling cocoa in one hand, his alarm clock in the other.

He warns after me, anxious, ineffectual. 'We'll talk about this in the morning!'

I slam my bedroom door, inconsiderate, avoiding the hour and the fact that everyone else has retired to bed.

Time to consider. Time to undress. Time to lie on my bed in the stripe of a moonbeam, to think and think through the muddle of drink and consternation.

First time. First sex. Uncomfortably disappointing. Under a pile of coats in a spare bedroom. I'd been thinking too much Hemingway and not enough O-level biology. The earth had not moved; the coats had been disturbed at the climax, when someone had reclaimed the top one and forced the disappointing and messy finish. Embarrassed, they had mumbled an apology and left the room, hurriedly. Rapid readjustment of clothing. I recalled thinking that I was no longer a virgin; that I had been expecting to be consulted before losing it.

In my mind I can still see Reuben; Reuben rolling to the floor, hazy, drunken Reuben, spent and uncaring, absorbed in his own needs, forgetful of mine. Pulling up the waist of his Levi jeans, he clumsily wiped himself on the bed counterpane before closing his fly zip and struggling to unsteady feet; he went out through the bedroom door, not giving me a second glance, disregarded, finished with. I heard the toilet door bang open, heard him kneel, heave, vomit into the pan; someone mocked him, someone joked that he was calling for his mate 'Huey', someone imitated the sounds of his alcohol-poisoned gut wrenching over the bowl. Brian's voice. Brian joking. Sober Brian. Irritatingly predictable Brian. Safe Brian. Brian who thought the first time would be his. I waited; waited until I heard them tumble together, waited until they were mates together, falling in matey unison downstairs, joking together down to the music below. I waited for the party voices greeting Brian, asking where he had been, taking the piss because he had been made to take his mum to Brighton instead of arriving earlier with me, asking where I was. I listened to his search among the battered 'Party Four' cans, his inability to find some remnants of stale ale; I avoided answering him when I heard him call my name. Finally he called out to anybody listening that he was going to the off-licence before they closed, hoping to get some more beer. I heard the street door slam, the predictable car grind into second gear, the engine jerk in its attempt to move up the road, the stops and spluttering starts, the final pulling away, the expected soot-filled pop from the rusty exhaust pipe.

I lie on my bed in the zebra stripes of the moonlight and think of how dirty I feel. The sort of a best friend I am. The sort of almost-fiancée. I don't want to think of Reuben but frequently he flickers across my mind, like a ghoul from a 'B' film, the Boris Karloff of my half-dreams. Lying on my bed in the moonlight, wanting to be crisp and clean, wanting a Persil moment to make things go white. I get up. I go to the bathroom.

It is the middle of the night and I run a bath. I am running a bath in a household where baths are only run during the early evening, in a household where baths are regular and routine and monitored by the electricity meter. I want it to run secretly, silently. It chooses not to. Choosing to gurgle and chase like a maniac's laugh, the water dribbles over the water-stain on the enamel beneath the polished taps; the impossible-to-remove stain that my mum tries to Ajax to perfection and my dad douses with some noxious substance that he secretes from his workplace; a brown-centred, mustard-edged stain, like the one that has appeared in the crotch of my panties. The water collects in lethargic bubbles, popping effortlessly to the tranquil surface. I reach for the birthday bath salts, turning the jar open-mouthed over the water to pour rose-coloured crystals; baby pink trickling down in tiny plimping puffs of scented steam. I swish the soda-soaked rain drops; they spiral into flamingo-pink rings, soothing over the yellow-stained enamel and concealing the brown oval in candy-floss froth. The room fogs with steam, steam that clings in tearful rivulets to the cold mirror glass and the darkened window pane with the icy moon haze. I close off the tap.

Slipping out of my clothes, I submerge my whole body completely under the water, hot to the touch and cold on the rinsing; I cleanse my back, my arms, under my buttocks, between my thighs, drawing out the badness and dissolving the dissipating mistakes in the healing water. I let my hair fan out in strands; it drifts in a wiry raft to the bath sides and I close my eyes; I open my lips and I fall under the rosy scum that sweetly smells of carnations. The cocoon of water covers me in weightlessness; I am floating in a fuchsia sea edged with strawberry, losing control of my limbs and filling up with a translucent calm.

My dad's voice brings me into a sudden chilled sitting position. 'Are you in there? You're not having a bath! It's the middle of the night!'

The water slops. Cold scum, cold surface. Goose-bumps rise on my partially submerged body, wet rat's tails on my back. I call back, trying to sound weak. 'I'm not well!'

My dad coughs his Woodbine cough. 'You'd better not be drunk!'

My mum's voice calls, bedroom-heavy, irritable, desperately seeking to regain her sleep. 'It's women's stuff, Frank! Leave the girl alone!'

My dad mutters his obedience and I hear their bedroom door close on his grumbling. It muffles and then stops.

I rise up cold, a scum-soaked Venus in a miserable damp towel; no opportunity to dry my hair, unless I want to risk waking the house, which I don't. I pull up the bath plug and watch the gurgle of candy water whirl away until the permanent water stain is revealed, the dead bath salts foaming grey in the bottom of the bath.

I stand and reflect. Messy stain. Messy bath. Messy life.

CHARLOTTE GÄBLER-GOES
When He Met Death

THE WALLS CAN'T DULL the sound of sirens down in the streets, and the half-closed shutters can't keep away the blue lights, forcing through panel cracks, penetrating his sleep like sharp, hot needles. Something is always happening outside. Yet tonight, the presence of a police commando just down the stairs is especially unsettling. Julian gets that quiet humming of foreboding, clenching and unclenching inside his chest; the notion that tonight, something special must have happened, or is about to happen; something that he, for once, can't hide from behind locked doors and barred windows.

He is unsure whether it's the lights or the noise keeping him awake. He should be used to it by now. The cardboard boxes that littered the apartment in the beginning are long unpacked and stashed away between a chest of drawers and the moist wall of his bedroom. He shifts from one side of the bed to the other. The thin white covers stick to his sweat-coated skin like a shroud. If he lies still for a moment, he might pass for a corpse, with paper-screen skin and withered-grape eyes.

He's more asleep during the day, staring at smart-boards and the backs of classmates' heads through lids he can barely keep open; adding a few words to his half-finished homework. He's wading through an oil spill that clings to his shoulders and nestles in his veins.

A few nights ago, he came home late. His dad was watching one of those documentaries. On screen: oil-clotted seagulls that couldn't even open their beaks to cry any more. 'Poor things,' his dad had said and taken another sip of soda. 'Remember when we went fishing on that barge in Antor, and those bloody bastards tried to nick our catch? They're persistent little buggers. When they can fly, that is. Even tried to pluck the fish right from David's hands.'

Julian still keeps the photograph they took that day, buried six feet under old newspaper clippings and failed class tests. It shows Julian and David, his older brother, with David's right arm wrapped around Julian's shoulders, a giant codfish squeezed beneath his left.

Impressive, how depression can be triggered by one event and then develop into something completely independent. Julian probably had the genetic disposition.

He hears a dog whining on the other side of the wall. A constant, pathetic wail, not unlike the sirens outside. The dirty brown crossbreed belongs to the couple living next door. They're cooking up meth in their kitchen to pay the rent. When they're not sure they did it right, they feed it to the dog. Sometimes Julian hears their dog wailing, sometimes he hears them fucking. It's not much of a difference, sound-wise. When they're at it, Julian imagines him taking her from behind, his breath coming out in long rasps and grunts. She's a white trash runaway, eyes set deep in the sockets, black-rimmed like only those of drug-addicts. He's an ex-cop. Lovely irony, Julian thinks.

Nobody knows what he did. Some say it was theft, others say it was rape that cost him the badge.

Julian is staring at the bedroom ceiling. There's a dark patch of mould in one corner. He imagines the tiny particles coming off the wall and flying through the air, attaching themselves to the sides of his lungs. What will kill him first? This or the smoking? Or will it be a bullet to the brain? In Chroma, only sixty per cent of the population dies of a natural cause.

Or maybe he'll die from insomnia, if those damned sirens don't shut up any time soon.

What the hell is going on down there – another drug bust? He flips the covers aside, gets up and walks over to the window, through the dusky glow from his minicom plugged into its charging station and the screen of his PC that runs the home page of the city's newspaper. 'After three months of investigation, the death of nineteen-year-old D. Marran is finally declared an accident, clearing delegate Teon

Konrad of all charges,' it reads. It has done so for the past few days, making sure everyone gets the message. Or maybe there's just nothing new to report, who knows? Julian switches the screen off.

He pulls the shutters apart with a finger and looks down into the streets, where another police car rushes past, siren distorted by the Doppler effect. Next, there's an ambulance, howling asynchronously, and voices shouting. It makes the skin of his arms break out in goose-bumps. He looks through the window at an awkward angle, forehead pressed against the shutter panels, with his breath fogging the glass. From here, he can only see the tops of the cars, not the actual scene.

From the rack in the kitchen, he takes a coat. He bumps his toe on a bookshelf, grimacing in pain as he stumbles through the semi-dark, not wanting to turn on the light and wake his dad, who is asleep on the couch, the TV in front of him still running the muted news channel. He does that a lot recently, exchanging the comfort of his bed for the company of the CBN newscasters.

The coat smells strange, as if it has hung unworn for a long time, but Julian shrugs into it anyway and steps out on to the rusty landing that overhangs the street, sticking to the apartment wall like metal pipes protruding from a sunken shipwreck. This is Lower Level 1: decrepit old buildings from which the government has withdrawn the funding to renovate. There's an ever-present stench of homelessness and unemployment. Some people like it this way. They say it's refreshingly honest, compared to the hypocritical glamour of the upper levels.

Julian has been to the upper levels before. He knows that 'glamour' is an accurate description. When the sun hangs low, its light cascades down the window panes and makes the city glow like a freshly cut diamond, all sharp edges and steep, clean planes. Sometimes it even shines down here, slivers of light darting through the transparent floors of the three platforms above.

'Hello, neighbour.' The ex-cop's wife is leaning on the railing in front of their barred living room window, warming herself on the bright square she's clutching in her freezing hands. 'Chilly night,' she says, without looking up from the minicom.

'Hi,' Julian says.

'You can't sleep.'

'Right,' Julian says.

'I can't sleep either. At night. Night makes me paranoid,' she says. For a second, she looks up at him. 'It's not even dark,' she laughs, exposing a row of uneven teeth. She points at the surrounding buildings, lit windows and flashing billboard screens. 'I should be afraid of the dark, not of the night. What is night without dark?'

How can she be afraid of the dark, of dying, of anything, Julian briefly wonders, gazing at her sunken eyes. What has she got to lose?

'Statistically speaking, night is still when most murders are committed,' he says. He has to bend far over the metal railing before he can see what's going on down in the streets.

'Oh, you better not look at that,' the woman says. 'It's nasty.'

By now, there are a dozen police cars plus the ambulance crowded around the scene. Two paramedics come running, carrying a stretcher, but it's probably too late; Julian can see that from afar. Judging by the clothes, it could have been a construction worker. Judging by the blood, he must have come all the way down from the upper levels. One would think that they'd have security belts, dangling from skyscrapers and climbing around scaffolding like that.

The man's cracked-open skull spills his brain out on to the concrete.

Julian has never seen a real human brain before. This one is barely identifiable, compressed by the forceful impact. There's much more blood than he'd have imagined someone's head contained, and there's a slight pulling sensation inside Julian's stomach when he looks at it, even from afar. It's not unpleasant, though. Maybe listening to your father's horror stories as a prison warden hardens you against the horrors of discovering that people are, after all, just flesh, blood and bone.

There's barking. Not the neighbours' dog. Now it's stray dogs, circling like sharks in an ocean of asphalt, hiding in the shadows of the cars. If they could, they would get a hold of that brain and lap it all up with their craggy tongues. Eat or be eaten.

'Nasty, I told you so.' She sniffs a bit of snot back up her nose. 'But great. That stuff makes good movies.'

The trickle of blood beneath them slowly begins to form rivulets, leaking into the drain that will carry it to Ground Level, to 'The Pit', to God knows where.

The sensible thing would be to get back inside. Look away from the train wreck. Move on, there's nothing to see here.

'Fuck it, I'm going down there.' Julian says, pulling the coat tighter around him.

'Really gets you off, doesn't it?' she says.

It takes Julian about a minute to descend the spiral staircase of the apartment complex. By then, the paramedics have already heaved the body on to the stretcher and lifted it into the ambulance. But the blood and brains are still there.

This could have been me, Julian thinks, contemplating the smudge of human remains beyond the fluttering police tape.

'Stay back.' One of the officers shoves him away from the tape, but Julian stays and looks.

A few times, when he'd skipped lessons and gazed into the depths of the city from above, he'd thought about jumping, flying for a while with wings outstretched, unglued. Before his eyes the buildings zoomed past in a blur of steel and glass. The air slipped into his clothes and tore at them, determined to touch the skin that coated his breathing body. There was a beating heart inside, beating frantically, so very much alive. Funny, how he'd be most alive the seconds before he died.

He doesn't tell his therapist about it, no, he doesn't want a pill prescription on top of being filed as suicidal. Because he is. He admits that to himself.

When he's sitting in the big squashy leather chair that practically devours him, he feels tiny again, like a bird without feathers. She sits in a twin chair, facing him, and he expressionlessly stares at the clipboard she never uses, placed on her lap, while he talks. He uses up the hour that is paid for by his father's extra shifts and his brother's leftover money. Above the clipboard, a green woollen sweater invades his field of vision, with an enormous gem pendant dangling between her flaccid tits.

'I know you're going to think I'm this pathetic little boy who can't get over what's happened to him,' he said to her the last time.

'Why do you think that? It's only been three months,' she said, pen hovering a centimetre above the paper.

The voices of the two officers pull Julian from the depths of his memory. 'Finally, forensics will be here in two minutes,' one of them says. He sounds vaguely familiar, but in the shadow of the ambulance, his face isn't really distinguishable. The other officer is casually leaning on the door of a police car, in a way he probably thinks looks cool, examining the dirt beneath his fingernails.

'I don't think we need forensics here,' he says. 'Let's just pack up and leave.'

The first officer steps into the police lights. They flash across his face in an even rhythm, drawing a prominent nose, a moustache, and grooves around his mouth, which he has pressed to a thin line. Julian realises, with a jolt, that he knows this man. Yes, it's the same mouth. The same despicable cleft in a face as if carved from wood. It opens a crack to say: 'Fortunately you're not the one giving orders.'

Unmistakeable. It's one of the officers who worked on David's case. What was his name? Schuster? Steiner? Julian remembers how he had been the one so keen to get rid of Julian and his father. It had been all 'Here, fill this form,' 'Put your signature,' and 'We're done with.'

Julian doesn't want to be seen, is about to turn around, pop up his collar and leave, but Woodface gets to him first, crossing the tape.

'Wait there, kid,' he says and advances on Julian in determined strides. 'How old are you?' he asks, looking Julian up and down with narrowed eyes, two slits like longish knotholes.

'Can't be older than seventeen,' the other one says.

Julian shrugs. 'What's it to you?' He keeps his head low, looking at the blood-soaked pavement and the dancing blue.

'Let's see some ID.' Woodface grabs the front of his coat, forcing Julian to push forward the little plastic card. 'Sixteen,' he says.

'I was just going home,' Julian explains.

'Of course.' Woodface sneers, still examining the card between his fingers. 'Marran?' A shadow of understanding crosses his face. 'You're the other Marran kid,' he says, tilting Julian's chin upward. Julian swats the unwelcome hand away, takes a step backwards.

'Are you serious?' the second officer says, joining them. The two gawp at him as if he is an oddity for display, as he has been for the past couple of months. It's making a hot bile-like burn slither down his throat, and he clenches his fingers into fists inside his coat pockets.

'It must be a relief, now that the case is closed,' the second one says.

'For whom?' asks Julian through gritted teeth. For them, of course. They don't have to deal with David's absence, they only had to sniff around Konrad's house and clear him. Respect the delegate's privacy, while no one respected his. Julian snatches the ID back from Woodface's fingers. 'Tell me,' he says, restraining himself the best he can, 'what kind of accident made my brother drop dead in the middle of Teon fucking Konrad's living room floor?'

The officers stay silent like two unmoving blocks of concrete. He has asked all of these questions before.

Paragraph 465 states that information within the merits of the law about members of the senate may not be disclosed to the public, if such information could be used in calumniation.

'You're just a bunch of useless pencil-pushers,' Julian says, turning his back to them.

Paragraph 547 states that defamation of a civil servant on duty is punishable by law.

Julian runs.

'Now, wait here, kid!'

They come after him. He quickens his pace, getting further and further away from the apartment complex. He hadn't wanted to say it.

'Don't make us use force,' Woodface calls.

And Julian stops. His hands are positively shaking now. He turns around, looks up at them.

'You should better watch your tongue, and watch your nose. Don't stick it into things which are none of your business,' Woodface says. 'Or you might just suffer the same fate as your hot-headed brother.'

This is it for Julian. 'What fate?' he barks. 'An accident? An accident that only looks like one?'

'You don't have any proof,' the second officer says, coming even closer, stretching out a hand for Julian's coat. But he ducks away, slips between their tree-trunk bodies and runs. Runs fast, runs away from the scene.

He remembers so well. He remembers the closed casket, the screeching of the gears straining to move it into the incinerator. The hiss of the incinerator doors, obscuring the casket from view, and the rustle of a 2,000-degree fire.

Nothing can bring back the dead, he knows that. No one can rise from the ashes.

He wishes David were completely dead. But no, it's like they say: a part of them lives on inside you, like a small tumour, gnawing at you and sucking the marrow from your bones to make them brittle and frail. And when you try to move on, step by step, setting one foot in front of the other, the arch of your foot will splinter and break.

The David Julian knew didn't have any enemies, not that you need any to die a violent death here. Then again, Julian hadn't seen much of him the six months prior to the accident. Murder, he corrects himself. If that's what it was. If it wasn't, why couldn't anyone tell him the truth? He'd probably never find out. This is not some kind of mystery movie. This is his life, and in life the past just stays where it is, out of reach, unsolved and incomprehensible. Until you wrap up the memory, stuff it inside a box and push it to the very back of your mind, from where it'll sometimes emerge to taunt and laugh at you.

He listens to the beat of his feet, listens for a sign of bones breaking. In his imagination, the soles of his shoes throw out sparks where they scrape the stained ground. He passes 'Live the good life. LL2 apartments', 'Join Myfit today', and 'The Jewel of "The Pit": Gamble Gambit' flashing across the LED-coated walls of deserted alleyways. A manky cat hastily scrambles into a pair of dumpsters cramped with instant-noodle boxes and protein bar wrappers as he approaches. He trips, falls, scrapes his knee on a rusty pipe jutting out from the wall, and forcibly throws up into one of the dumpsters. He'd feel a bit sorry for the cat, who's screeching at him with her fur standing on end, if he wasn't doubled over, clutching his stomach and coughing with threads of vomit dripping from the angles of his chapped lips. He spews out a couple of undigested pieces of the pizza he had for lunch. For once, he thinks, he's able to show an appropriate reaction.

He tries to get to his feet, tentatively supporting himself on the rim of the dumpster, but suddenly there is a small prick of pain, something cold hitting the back of his neck, and he winces away from it.

'Now, you probably don't want to do that. This is a gun I'm holding to your head,' a man's voice says. Julian has never heard the voice before: it's gruff and impatient. He tries to turn around, but is held in place by a push of the barrel into his neck. The pressure must surely leave an indentation on the skin.

'Get his ID, will you?'

He feels a pair of small, slender hands patting the sides of his coat and jeans, then extracting the enforced plastic card from his pockets.

'Confirmed. It's the Marran boy.' It's a woman's voice, sleek, unremarkable. If he's going to die here, he won't have time to create a profile anyway, so the details don't really matter. But still he thinks about them, puzzled and curious as is only natural, for once. They don't belong to the police, Julian is sure of that. But what do they want? Why him?

'Served on a silver platter. Who'd have thought?'

The tip of a boot hits Julian's spine, and he keels over again. His hands come up to grip for hold on the urine-stained ground, trailing through the dirt and loose plastic. He tilts his head upward, looking across three transparent levels of city jungle, air tunnels, glass lifts, cableways and balcony plantations, smudgy bits of laundry dangling from window ledges.

It's life, the incredible filth of it, crawling and creeping inside a termite mound of steel.

ALEX FLATT
Fleet

W HEN THE DELUGE *subsided, the land had been rubbed smooth.
    Every hole and crevice, every recess and pit, filled by the black waters
and the death they had brought with them.*

The waters had travelled down from the north-eastern reaches of the
Old City. They had oozed like tar over Hampstead leaving the freshly
hewn Parliament Island in their wake. The torrent had filled the ponds,
forcing the clean spring of the old river down into the murk, surging
into the tunnels and vaulted halls that had remained still, but for a
trickle, for three centuries. The devastation had recharged the Fleet.

The first wave had brought only wreckage, shards of what were
once possessions and splinters of the apparatus of day-to-day life.
Objects, once mundane, were imbued with violence and destruction,
window glass had cut people down, abandoned cars had smashed and
pulverised everyone in their path as they cascaded down the valley to
the Thames edge to meet the waters racing west.

It was here, at the spot where the Black Friary had once stood, that
the boundary of the devastation had formed. The sheer volume of the
grim waters filling Bazalgette's tunnels had forced their way up
through the herringbone brick into the basements of buildings, up
stairwells and lift shafts, up through layers of wood and tile and carpet,
up to be vomited out of windows and doorways and cracks in the brick.

The black soup had spewed forth from the masonry of High Holborn and Ludgate Hill out to meet the water and wreckage rolling over the banks that once restrained the Thames.

The second wave brought bodies. Bloated corpses marinated in the filth, collections of limbs wrapped in bloodied, tattered rags that were no longer recognisable as anything human.

By now the old river was open again, a fire-break to limit the damage done to the institutions of the west. The dam of mangled wreckage that formed a makeshift levee on the western bank was peppered with rotting corpses grounded on the bonnets and roofs of upturned cars, slumped on the mud banks, snagged and skewered on sections of mangled iron railing.

The stench became unbearable. The reek of slowly putrefying flesh mingled with the acrid smoke from the fires that raged in Hackney and Limehouse.

Looting began almost immediately, the mob emboldened by the absence of any sense of control. For a few days soldiers had come in helicopters and boats from the north but they retreated in the face of overwhelming odds. There was simply nothing to be done here and resources were needed elsewhere. When the supermarkets and corner stores had been emptied, homes were opened up. The comfortable hives of the middle classes that occupied the spaces between the old estates were taken first. The more fortunate residents fled, some made it west, those less able were burned where they fell, or else tossed into the black waters. Some, wily enough with properly adjusted survival instincts, gave up what they had and were absorbed into the mob; a single organism of violence and destruction, born from the chaos.

As softer targets dwindled, the power struggles and in-fighting began. The decaying concrete towers of Clapton, Homerton and Dalston became fortresses, each an urban fiefdom presided over by the strongest and most heavily armed. By the second month the war in the Upper East Fleet had taken hold. Battlements of contorted double-deckers and burnt-out cars were erected, with the now toxic mud providing a rich mortar. Castellations of broken glass adorned balconies and walkways, with armaments stockpiled to defend newly claimed territories. These were the first images of a conflict that would become a cursed inheritance for any unlucky enough to be born into the New City.

The third wave was the most devastating, coming, as it did, as plans were being laid for stabilisation and eventual repair. It had seemed pure in comparison to what had come before, with almost passive intent – a great cleansing torrent of silver and white sweeping through the detritus. The effluent and carcasses were washed downstream to the Thames confluence, confirming the terrain of the New City as the great alluvial tide swept through the streets.

There was no way back now and the decision to abandon was finally taken, quietly, in some distant office of the emergency government in the west. The artifice that help was on its way was maintained; the hastily erected bullhorns on the western reach repeated their reassurances hourly for the first few months. Supplies appeared in abundance, ferried across on pulley-skiffs, but it was the make-up of the pallets and crates that betrayed the long-term plan for the East Fleet.

Livestock first: pigs, goats, sheep, chickens; then tools, plastic sheeting, water butts, ploughs, shovels, generators, timber, endless pallets of tinned and processed food, fishing nets, welding masks, sheet steel, rivet guns, gas cylinders and grossly inadequate medical supplies. These were not temporary tools to see the East Fleet through the approaching winter, these were the apparatus of a burgeoning new state. Within the geographies of the Old City, the East Fleet was on its own. Quietly, the New City was born.

1

The column of guards, black-clad in trench coats and oily sou'westers, emerged from the stairwell on the thirteenth floor of the Canary. Thuds and muffled shouts from the lift shafts and corridors were so familiar a sound during the first hours of the day that their frequency no longer registered with the residents.

On the floor above, bruised morning light dragged itself through the windows, casting shadows of aluminium frames over the sleeping-bag-strewn office floor. Amorphous, down-clad maggots shifted and groaned, making the sounds of the early morning. Drench sat at the window ledge, the last watch of the night, looking down to the basin below and across to the yellow peaks of the dome beyond. Skiffs and rafts chugged and skittered over the water displacing flotsam and screeching gulls, carrying a cargo of workers returning from night shifts in the basements and sewers of the West Fleet.

Drench scanned the boats below, idly hoping to spot Connie amongst the distant specks. As he pressed his forehead to the dusty glass he was momentarily aware of a raised arm in the reflection.

2

The wind was sharp off the water and cut through the thin muslin scarf tied around Whittington's neck. He thumbed the clutch of crumpled chits buried deep in his pocket, seventy-two out tonight, maybe sixty-five back tomorrow – any more would be considered a great success.

The job of a bailiff was simple enough, count them out, count them in, any that don't return, find them and bring them back. Fast. Whittington was good at his job; he couldn't stop the runners from attempting escape but he always brought them back. Only twice had he needed to cross the water himself and only once in twenty years had he needed to kill anyone.

Ready access to violence was the primary tool of the bailiffs. As an apprentice Whittington had been shown thirty-six different techniques to break an arm; by age eighteen he knew ten different methods for non-fatal torture. Despite this schooling in brutality, his exemplary retrieval rate was almost entirely a result of good contacts, genuine admiration for the boldness of his quarry and a calm but menacing restatement of the facts at the proper time. An indeterminate stint in Barbican Gaol is always preferable to excruciating torture and death.

He turned right off the plank-walk, relieved to have put some distance between his nostrils and the stench of the river, and cut through the rat-run of narrow, mud-lined alleys that led up to Ludgate Hill and the gentle rise of St Paul's.

He had often thought it strange that he never became accustomed to the smell, the essence of the East Fleet. It pervaded everything; it was in his clothes, in his hair and on everything else he owned, but this fierce assault on the senses had long become an accepted norm, seemingly to all but Whittington. He had never known any different, but to him the miasma was a blanket to stifle possibility beyond simple survival. The reek was a toxin to repress hope.

The courtyard of St Paul's was a cauldron of aggression and frustration as always. The mêlée of refugees down from Hackney and Clapton were packed in and desperate, fleeing the latest rounds of tit-for-tat street fighting. In truth, there was nothing the Magistrate's Office could do for them save the meagre handouts of stale bread and plastic sheeting, always offered with the suggestion to move north where they might find some space in the shanties around Hornsey and Muswell Hill; eventually they would all take their chances on the slopes.

Skirting the throng and edging his way along to the entrance at the south vestibule, Whittington passed the guards with a nod.

Inside, the marble-floored atrium was spotless as always; no hint of the effluence and squalor outside was ever allowed to penetrate the inner sanctum. At the foot of the spiral staircase, leading up to the dome, two guards stood sentinel beside a large wooden chest, painted with a crude depiction of Noah's Ark. As Whittington strode toward the guards, two char-girls emerged from the shadows of the great circular hall and scurried into step behind him, sweeping and mopping in his wake, removing evidence of the streets from the pink stone.

'Boots!' barked one of the guards.

Already bending down to unbuckle the straps of his gaiters, Whittington prized his boots off, taking the carrier bag liners with them, and dropped the whole muddy bundle into the painted chest which was promptly slammed shut by the guard.

The doorway to the Magistrate's Office was low, and Whittington had to stoop to manoeuvre his six-foot frame into the room. The vast office was cold and shrouded in an oppressive pewter light that dulled its grand appointments. The walls were lined with books, each one individually encased in a clear plastic bag. One large window, set between the shelves opposite the door, let the dirge of the outside in. The deep red carpet had the quality of a manicured lawn, each fibre seemingly in perfect alignment to the next. A stripe of glossy white linoleum cut through the centre of the crimson expanse and at the end of this plastic pathway, behind an imposing oak desk, picked out by a shaft of dusty light from the window, sat Beade the Magistrate.

'Sit, sit.'

Beade opened the thick ledger in front of him and pushed his half-moon glasses up the bridge of his nose.

'Now, how many out?'

'Seventy-two.'

'Good, good.'

He scribbled the figure in the book, 'And we'll have seventy-two back on Monday?'

'Unlikely, sir.'

'Yes, well, they all come back eventually . . . One way or another.'

Beade carefully closed the ledger and with sharp fingertips removed his glasses, gently placing them alongside his pencil at precise right angles to the book. He blinked unnaturally, screwing his eyes tight shut, and proceeded to tap the desk lightly with the palm and then knuckles of his right hand and then again with his left. He shot a concerned look at Whittington, helpless to his tick.

'Of course, I didn't ask you here just for your numbers.'

'No sir.'

'Fact is, we have something of a problem.'

Whittington watched as he unfolded a small sheet of plastic, smoothed it out on to the desk and gestured to one of the guards who marched down the linoleum channel carrying with him a stained cardboard box. The box was placed carefully on the plastic. Beade edged away, shifting uncomfortably in his chair. He repeated his palm and knuckle routine, this time adding an alternating wink to the coda. Averting his eyes, he extended a trembling index finger toward the box.

'Please, if you would, Mr Whittington.'

Fixed in his chair, his eyes locked on the twitching Beade, Whittington inhaled the familiar stink of the river, cut through with rotting meat. He noted the dimensions of the box and the damp, rust-coloured stains at its base.

'Head?'

Beade nodded and blinked an affirmation, bony hand now clasped across his mouth and nose. Whittington sat back in his chair and raised his eyebrows in anticipation of the story that would accompany the gruesome package.

The retrieval of a head from the waters, although unpleasant, was not an altogether uncommon occurrence. Body parts were a frequent fixture of the lower reaches of the Fleet, whether risen from the depths, dislodged by some unexpected movement below the surface, or borne downstream, dumped by combatants and muggers further up the course. Most were removed quietly by the guards and burnt in the pyres. Identification, let alone investigation, would be an impossible undertaking, even if the will existed.

'This is the twelfth we've had delivered this month,' offered the Magistrate through gritted teeth, his knuckles white as he clenched sweating fists, wrestling his compulsion to repeat his hand ritual.

'Delivered?'

'They've been sending them back on the work boats, with instructions for delivery directly to this office. This is the first we've been able to identify, Constance Renthrew. Please, if you would, Mr Whittington.'

The sharp digit extended again in the direction of the box.

Whittington hauled his bulk from the chair and pulled his scarf up over his mouth as a makeshift filter. Placing palms flat on the desk he leant over the open box.

Matted red hair tangled round a bloated blue-green neck with the texture of decaying leather. The raw wound where the head had been severed was tacky and yellowing, at its centre a bleached white cross-section of spinal column. Face down, the late Constance Renthrew had a strange serenity, the quiet and peaceful sleep of an exhausted child. The crown of her hair parted in a star shape and loose waves of auburn looped down to absent shoulders. There, at the base of her neck, where gold or silver had hung, was a crude tattoo carved in juvenile scrawl that read, 'Drench & Connie 14 Canary Luv u 4 Eva'.

Gazing at the ink, he felt a sudden compulsion to lift the head from the box, to look into the girl's eyes, to find a way to know her but he was simultaneously revolted by his desire to feel something for this wretched girl. He had long since learned to repress any sense of empathy.

He folded the flaps of the box inward and lowered himself back into his chair.

Beade stared at the oily palm prints further sullying the sanctity of his desk. Without shifting his gaze back to Whittington he muttered,

'We have her, er . . . known associates, of course. A boyfriend.'

'Sir?'

Whittington slouched into the chair, still unclear as to the part he had to play in all of this. It seemed likely that it would involve more than a simple recount of the week's missing. He swallowed the sense of impending dread at the imminent disruption to his routine.

'It won't do, Whittington, it won't do at all. Miss Renthrew here is the twelfth unaccounted this month. As far as Westminster is concerned that's twelve illegals that have made it through, twelve illegals that we have not retrieved, that *they* have not captured, living amongst them, using their resources, eating their food. Shitting in their streets, I dare say!'

Nostrils flared in disgust, Beade nudged the ledger across the desk with the tip of his pencil until it covered Whittington's greasy hand marks.

'Crossings will be closed, what little trade we have will cease, we will be set adrift, Whittington, no work parties, no credit, no salvation!'

'If she's dead she can hardly be considered a runner, sir.'

Beade shot Whittington a glare of pained contempt.

'The Lightermen were informed.' He carefully replaced the pencil at its right angle, calmer now but blinking unnaturally at the ledger.

'As you might imagine, there is some resistance to the idea that girls from the East Fleet are being . . .' He paused, swallowing and then regurgitating the word in a whisper, 'decapitated on their lunch breaks. This is on us, Mr Whittington. Westminster believes the heads are a ruse, a plot of our making to disguise our failings in keeping the runners in check.'

Whittington rubbed the coarse bristle under his chin with calloused knuckles and felt the muscles in his back tense. The west's assumptions of savagery in the East Fleet were often warranted but none the less a gross insult to all those attempting, against all odds, to retain some dignity and humanity in otherwise inhuman circumstances.

The idea that the torn-off heads of citizens were being procured, produced even, to disguise the failings of an impossible government, was entirely in line with the western image of apocalyptic self-consumption in the East Fleet. Stories expertly spun by propagandists in the news sheets of Marylebone and Soho, further chattered into reality by their fearful captive readership, saw the human waste of the east committing the most vile atrocities with nightly regularity. To their distant kin across the trench the monsters from the east were rapists, murderers, baby-eaters all.

'Naturally, you will be remunerated. Westminster has suggested two hundred stamps. I'd suggest you start with the boy: he and Miss Renthrew often worked the same cellars, a touching romance indeed. You'll find him in the Lock at Bank . . . Along with the rest of the heads, of course . . .'

The magistrate scribbled something on a small scrap of vellum, slipped it into a clear plastic wallet and handed it to Whittington.

'Give this to the guard.'

Whittington stared blankly at the note, 'Central Line.'

'I'm sorry, sir, I'm not entirely sure what you want me to do . . .'

'Your job, Whittington. Bring him back.'

The magistrate tapped his fingertips on the desk.

'The boyfriend?'

'The killer, Whittington. Bring back the killer.'

RENUKA DAVID

I Saw a Sunbird

I WAS ALLOWED to pack two of my toys for our Christmas holiday to Sri Lanka, but wanted to take more so my cousins and friends could see what I played with in England. My shoeflower-red pyjamas were still too long for me and I had to pull them up while I ran about collecting dolls and teddy bears. After emptying my cupboard and shelves on to the bed, putting big toys at the back and small ones at the front, I looked at everything to choose what to carry on the plane. Most of all, I wanted to take the walkie-talkie doll I'd just got for my seventh birthday. She was too tall to lie down in the holdall and had to sit with her head and chest sticking up. Dad wouldn't let me carry her like that. He wanted all zips closed and cases locked. I thought about pulling off her legs to make her fit in but Dad said he wouldn't fix her if I broke her again. I lifted her out with both hands and put her back on the bed then ran around choosing smaller toys until Mum called me from the hallway.

'Rohini,' she said. 'Are you dressed?'

'Nearly.'

She came thump, thump, thump, up the stairs. My heart started beating fast. I shut my bedroom door and stuffed my Sindy and Russian dolls into the holdall, pushing them near the bottom to make space for more toys and games. Mum's footsteps were getting louder and a floor-board creaked. She must have been on the landing. I shoved in my

Stylophone, a paint box and a ball of string for playing cat's cradle and then squeezed in a hot water bottle cover that looked like a dog, forcing it down so I could do up the zip. The door knob turned. I tried to close the holdall before Mum came in.

I was too late.

The door opened wide and she stood there, hands on hips, giving me a funny look. I looked back at her, as if I hadn't done anything wrong.

'Is there something you want to tell me?' she asked.

'No . . .'

I stood in front of the holdall. It was no use. She took it and emptied it on the bed. Out tumbled everything I'd packed.

'Two toys,' she said. 'We need space for all the clothes and gifts we'll bring back.'

'I can't separate them. They're a set.'

'I said only two.'

'You choose.'

She picked up my Sindy and Russian dolls and left the poor puppy dog behind.

'You've broken his heart,' I told her.

'It'll mend.' She kissed the top of my head. 'Off you go and wash.'

'Post has arrived,' Dad shouted from downstairs.

I jumped up and down. I'd been waiting days and days for a letter from my grandparents. I woke up early every morning to see if they'd sent me their news.

'Do you think Appa and Amma will have written to me?' I asked Mum.

'The sooner you get dressed, the sooner you'll find out.'

I ran to the bathroom and washed with the rosy-pink soap because Mum would feel it afterwards to see if it was wet. She could also tell if I just threw water at the soap and didn't use it properly.

As soon as I had my vest and jungies on, I tried to go downstairs. Mum pointed at the skirt and jumper she'd put on my bed. God gave me a mother to look after me, but he never meant her to make me get fully dressed when I was in a hurry to do something else. She watched as I went towards the door. Her mouth wasn't smiling and she pushed her eyebrows up, so I gave in and put the skirt and jumper on. It wasn't going to be for long, anyway – the next day I was going to be in Sri Lanka, wearing summer dresses and not winter clothes.

I sang, 'Jingle bells, jingle bells. Join in, Mum.'

'Later, girl.'

When I was older and had children of my own, I was going to let them do anything they liked, even if they wanted to sing while getting dressed. I wriggled while Mum tried to plait my hair, so she put it in two bunches instead. Her hair was long as well because we both liked to look Sri Lankan.

'You can go,' she said. 'That's all I can do while you're like this.'

I rushed down to search the post on the hall table. Sometimes my grandparents sent an envelope with a letter and postcard of a sunbird inside, sometimes they sent a thin blue airmail form.

'Is there anything for you?' Dad asked from the sitting room.

'They're all for Mr and Mrs Palar.'

'Keep looking. You never know.'

I read names on the envelopes, letter by letter, but all the post was for my parents. There was nothing for me. Appa and Amma had forgotten to write. I wanted to hear their news then, not wait until I saw them in Colombo. Then, just as I was about to give up, there it was, right at the bottom of the pile: an airmail with my name on the front and theirs on the back. I hugged it to my heart and gave it to Dad while he sipped a cup of tea.

'Sure you don't want to open it?' he asked me.

'I might tear it.'

After he put his cup on the nest of tables, I jumped on to his lap and leaned my head against his shoulder.

'Do you want to try and read it?' he asked.

'I can only read proper writing, not Appa's scribble.'

He laughed and kissed the top of my head.

I touched his long fingers as he ran them across the top of the letter.

'Mum says you could be a concert pianist if you want.'

He thought about it but didn't say anything.

'She said you became a lawyer, to send burglars to prison so they won't break into our house and steal my toys.'

He took a slow sip of tea, licked a drop off the corner of his mouth, and began reading. His voice was quieter than when he read me bedtime stories.

14 December 1972
Dear pretty Rohini,
Your grandmother and I are very happy to know we'll see you soon. We miss you all and look forward every year to your Christmas visit. This holiday is going to be special because the Temple tree is full of flowers and a Loten's sunbird has made a nest in the top branches. Remember, darling girl, our family has always stayed together while there is a sunbird in the garden.

I crossed my fingers and made a wish for the bird to hang around so we could stay in Sri Lanka with my Appa and Amma forever. They sent me their love and said they were going to keep the letter short, or they wouldn't have any news to tell me when we arrived.

And don't worry about Saraswathie and the other servants. We're taking good care of them, although our new maid got homesick after a week and went back to Jaffna. So we've hired a houseboy from a family of Veddhas.

'What're they?' I asked Dad.
'They're the first people of Sri Lanka. They used to live in forests and caves and hunt for food. There aren't many left. They're disappearing fast.'
I hoped the houseboy wouldn't disappear before we arrived, so I could tell my friends I'd seen a Veddha.
'Did Appa and Amma go to the forest to find him?'
'Most Veddhas live in towns now. Only a few stay in the wild.'
'I'd like to go to the jungle.'
'Maybe we can take a trip there if we have time.'
Mum came in and sat next to us, saying, 'I've finished packing, Nathan.' She asked him to read the letter again but she didn't really listen; she looked at the bamboo wallpaper, then the stone-colour carpet. When he stopped reading, she said, 'I feel like I've forgotten to buy something.'

My father rolled his eyes. 'Good grief, Uma. We've a suitcase full of shirts and shoes to take for this person or that one.'

'Did you tell Tara we didn't get her fridge?'

'I'll enjoy telling her in person.'

Poor Tara Aunty. She can't have known a fridge was too big to put on a plane or she wouldn't have asked us to bring one. I hoped Dad wasn't going to be rude when he told her off for being silly, or she wouldn't invite us to her parties.

He was still holding the letter. He liked to read it to himself when he was on his own. Mum had to cheer him up afterwards with a cup of orange pekoe tea and a joke.

I couldn't stop thinking about our holiday and, with God's help, was going to do all I could to make it the best ever. 'I'm going upstairs,' I told my parents. I knelt at the foot of my bed, shut my eyes and put my hands together, thinking carefully about what I was going to say. The Lord was ninety-four years old and got grumpy if he was asked to do too much.

'Hello, God. I'll pray for the poor people tonight, and I know I'm not supposed to ask for myself but I'd like a few favours from you. They could be your Christmas present to me. First, could you tell your angels to keep the sunbird safe in Appa's garden so our family can stay together? And if it's not too much trouble, can you ask Jesus to keep an eye on Amma in case her arthritis is bad again? And then if you're not ill with flu, please tell the airport not to lose our suitcases as my presents are in there.'

I was also going to ask him to make Mum change her mind and let me pack more than two toys, but it wouldn't have worked because mothers can do what they want. I waited for him to tell me which of my favours he was going to say yes to. He didn't answer. He must have been in hospital having a knee operation. He was so old he should have retired, like Dad's boss, and let Jesus speak to children instead. I said the Lord's Prayer anyway, so he'd see I knew it by heart but instead of keeping my eyes shut, I peeped at the puppy dog Mum was making me leave behind. I was going to tell her she made him cry. I gave him a goodbye kiss and said I'd bring him a present from holiday.

*

Near the end of the plane journey to Colombo, I woke up to hear the pilot say, 'We're in Sri Lankan airspace.' I knew that meant we were flying over Sri Lanka but all I could see were clouds and you got those in England. When I saw the runway and palm trees that looked fuzzy in the heat, I jiggled in my seat. I'd already changed into summer clothes like the other passengers so we could begin our holiday as soon as we landed. Once the seatbelt sign went off, everybody jumped up, grabbed coats and bags from overhead lockers and pushed their way up the aisle. As I tried to squeeze past Mum she put a hand on my shoulder and said, 'Let Dad go first.' We said thank you and goodbye to the air stewardesses, who looked pretty in blue uniform and red lipstick, then we marched off to pick up our luggage. I kept running ahead in the airport. Dad kept calling me back. My hand was hot and sticky on the handle of my holdall, but it didn't matter. I loved seeing brown people everywhere and signs in squiggly writing.

I hopped around while we waited at the merry-go-round for our suitcases to turn up. When they did arrive, I went to climb on top of them for a ride, like at a funfair. Dad pulled me off and Mum tried not to laugh while she scolded me because a small boy was copying what I did.

Once I knew the airport hadn't lost my presents, I didn't want to stay any longer at Katunayake. I wanted to be on the way to Colombo, driving down country roads, watching car wheels kick up dust and people ride bicycles, carrying a friend on the handlebars. I wanted to drive down Perth Avenue to Appa's house, to climb the Temple tree outside my bedroom and find the Loten's sunbird, if it was still there. And I couldn't wait to say hello to Saras, to wear the shoeflower necklace she made every year for me from the bushes in Appa's front garden.

Our porter followed us as we went through customs to the meeting point. I searched the crowd left to right and back again but couldn't see my grandparents. Then, in the middle, a lady with grey hair waved madly.

'Amma, Amma,' I said, waving back.

Dad got to them first.

Appa held him tight. 'It's good to see you again, son.'

My grandmother was crying. I held her hand and said, 'We're here now.' She didn't speak while she dried her eyes with a white lace hanky she used for special occasions. I didn't think I should tell her she'd put on so much face powder that some had fallen on to her sari. Dad put an arm around her, not pressing hard, in case her arthritis was bad. We hugged each other for a few minutes until Appa moved away and said we should go. I'd hoped Saras might be at the airport but servants weren't allowed on family outings. I had to wait until we reached Appa's house to see my ayah.

After the porter put our suitcases in the boot, Mum tipped him thirty rupees. He looked at how much she gave him and said, 'Thank you, thank you,' while shaking his head from side to side. I'd done that at school once. My friends called me a nodding dog so I never did it again. The porter said, 'Thank you,' again to Mum.

Appa said, 'Uma, you gave him more than he gets in a month.'

'It was worth it, to see the look on his face.'

I tried to sit in the front seat of the car, but had to go in the back between Mum and Amma, away from the door. I leaned forward to watch a man climb a palm tree, the handle of a long knife in his mouth. He cut off broken branches then let them crash to the ground.

'That tree must have been damaged in yesterday's storms,' Amma said. 'This monsoon comes and goes.'

When I was older, I was going to climb a palm tree all the way to the top and when I was seventeen, I was going to do it with a knife in my mouth. I'd chop, chop, chop all the torn leaves and watch as they flew to the ground and landed on top of each other with a rustling noise. Then I was going to pick all the best coconuts and leave the rest to ripen.

Appa beeped a bullock cart in front of us but it didn't move to the side so he overtook it. I knelt on the seat to look behind at the driver. He stared ahead, as if he hadn't seen or heard us, then he spat out red betel he'd been chewing.

It was stuffy in the car. 'Can you wind down the window?' I asked Mum.

'We'll get grit in our eyes, sweetheart.'

The cold air blower that Dad turned on didn't help much. At Appa's house, if I was hot and Saras wasn't busy, she'd sit me on her lap to cool me with a wooden fan.

'Is Saras at home?' I asked Amma.

'Yes, child.'

We drove past a couple of villages then stopped at a crossroads. A beggar man with one hand tapped on my grandmother's window and frightened me. She pretended not to see him.

'It's better to give to places that help them,' she said.

I hoped someone would give him money to buy lunch.

All along the road were rows of huts with tin roofs, selling warm Fanta, Portello and king coconuts. Rich people never bought patties or Chinese rolls from them because they'd get an upset stomach.

'Are we there yet?' I asked.

'Nearly,' Dad said. 'This is Mount Lavinia.'

Appa's house was a bit farther along Galle road, past the Hindu temple that had a totem pole of gods on the roof. I wriggled when we turned into Perth Avenue, which had houses on one side and a field of palm trees on the other. When we went for walks, I stayed away from the field because a cobra lived there.

'Can you wind down the window?' I asked Mum. 'I want to smell the sea.' I sat on her lap and stuck my tongue out to taste the salt in the air.

As we turned into Appa's house at the end of the road, I saw Saras waiting for us on the front veranda. She looked as if she'd put on a new green sarong and blouse. I loved her as much as I did Mum and Dad and Appa and Amma but couldn't tell anyone. You weren't supposed to feel like that about servants, even if they were the same as family. As soon as the car stopped, I climbed out and ran to hug Saras round the knees. I didn't want to let her go. Her long, black plait was shiny with coconut oil, the last thing I used to smell when she put me to bed. Stroking my head, she spoke softly in Tamil. I pushed my face into her sarong and cried my eyes out. When I finished, she wiped my cheeks dry with thumbs that were rough from doing servant's work, and put a necklace of red shoeflowers over my head. The petals around my neck were soft, like a silk sari.

'I really love this,' I said.

SHIKO
The Dragon Outside

GIANNI ROLLS HIS HEAD back, laughs triumphantly, his thick wavy hair quivering in tune to the melody of his sound. I stand aghast, still in disbelief. I stare at the curious animal outside our kitchen, comfortably perched on the long porch that runs alongside the villa.

'My God,' I whisper.

Gianni stands proud, tall, behind me. I can feel his warmth, his strong male body behind my own. I am shaking inside. I know that no matter how still I stand, he knows this. Neither of us knows for sure if it his body against mine that causes this shimmering inside or if it is the magnificent mythical creature that stands proud too before us.

'Trust me.'

Gianni pulls me gently forward, his hand behind my shoulder blade, his body closely lined with mine. I step closer, away from his heat, hesitant to part with him, hesitant to move toward this ominous beauty before me. The Komodo dragon stares straight ahead, dead still, its glossy, dark eyes fixated and its resolve intent. It hears us and its bright head cocks sideways, staring directly at us. It is motionless for a moment, each party sounding out the other. With a flicker of red, its rounded ribcage and slender body weaves like a snake from side to side as it scurries off into the dry, brown bushes beside the porch and is gone.

I saw a dragon.

The hushed tone the house had taken on is broken by a satisfied voice behind me. Gianni releases my shoulders, walking towards the fridge. The touch of his fingers was heavy, weighted with all the things yet unexpressed. He drinks straight from the mouth of the juice bottle.

I have known Gianni for some time now. We connected the moment we met. He is older than I am. He often reminds me of this, that I am living the life of someone his age, and tells me to slow down, to take life in. I remind him that life does not often allow us such privileges as choice. Gianni is the heat in the pit of my stomach. He is the force that holds us all together in this villa, this group of wildly different people that somehow gels, fits together unpredictably like a temporary puzzle.

'*Que pasa aquí?*'

A gruff, yellow, smoke-coated lung coughs out from above. Javier's voice echoes as he descends the stairs from his hedonistic lair which overlooks the rest of the villa. He never fails to entertain us at night with a different woman. His browned Latin American skin looks polished in the light as he comes down the spiral staircase. It shines like ours in this climate. His muscles, like Gianni's, are moulded from hours of surfing.

At night Javier makes me laugh. We sit around our coffee table, the locus of our nightly discussions over wine, espresso and often stronger drugs. It is at night that I come into my own. It is when I best play my set of cards to match the rest, often beating them as if in a round of poker. We discuss everything from politics to philosophy to the things that aren't spoken of. I may be young, but my experience, history and education put me on an even footing. From the first night we spent together it was clear I was a fair match. It was on this first night that my lover Alain, Gianni's best friend, had set his sights on me. Gianni told me much later as if he had been keeping it from me, as if he had some reason to keep it to himself.

Javier chuckles below his breath, joining Gianni in this play of mockery. I had not believed until this moment that the dragon existed. The boys are affectionate but can sometimes be cruel. Alain is in the corner of the lounge, smiling. It is he who should put the fire in my belly but he does not. When we share the same bed at night it is not he who occupies my mind but his best friend in the next room.

On my arrival back here weeks ago, something strange happened between Alain and me, and that night our bed was not one where love was made. Since then, there has been something unspoken, something that stands between us, growing, like the slow piling up of invisible bricks on a wall. It is hard living between two countries and the expectations spun around Alain and me are like a slow, choking web that strangles the breath out of what we once had.

Andrea, our friend, knocks loudly. Exchanges pass in the form of 'Ciao' and 'Chau,' the Latin American bastardised version of the Italian greeting. Gianni saunters to the door where an argument ensues in that distinctive accent of Rome. I sense from the brevity of the visit and the tone of their voices that it has something to do with business. Andrea leaves. Gianni goes to the kitchen, fits together some apparatus. Alain is called in, and as he turns sideways, letting in the bright Asian sunshine, I can see what they are doing. I have never seen Gianni do this in the open kitchen before but I know enough to figure it out. As each of them chase the dragon, wafts of smoke curl in slow motion as they reach for the ceiling and disperse in the bright light.

'You want a little?' Alain's outstretched arm beckons, his hand turned downward in a way I like. It reminds me of the same polite gesture used back home. The downward-turned hand puts me at ease but as I walk over a fight has already begun. Alain's hand is slapped away – loud exclamations and wild hand gestures are being made. Gianni is incensed and they are engaged in an exchange I do not understand. They speak Spanish, the language from which I am excluded in this home.

Javier stands aside and stays out of it, but he clearly comprehends what is going on. It is his language being spoken. It is his language that is most often used here when English is not. It is the common denominator between them, from which I am excluded. Beneath the surface I always feel it as though someone is gently pinching my heart. I want to pull him aside but the pressure in the air has mounted and I stay still.

'She is not a child, you know! *Putain*!' Alain walks off.

Gianni is protective of me. I don't always appreciate it. Until this point I had not realised that it was the opium dragon that they chase. What we share in the evening at coffee table discussions is something entirely different. It is designed to stimulate the mind, the senses. The dragon I chase adds fire to our banter and comes only from this country. I know it only by its local name and it is only here that I have recently acquired a taste for it.

I stare out of the large kitchen window at the sea of rice fields around us. They shimmer beautifully in the sunlight and I cannot help but feel elated, despite what has just taken place. Wires have been carefully mapped across the landscape and hanging from them are tin cans with rattles attached at the centre. Early every morning, women stand at the end of the junctions to shake the wires; live human scarecrows who spread the tinkling of rusty metal, the sound of a new day.

The afternoon is warm and I head for the pool. The rush of water caresses every inch of my skin. I love this place and these people, they are my family now. Pushing off the wall beneath the surface of the water, I take long breaststrokes across the length of the pool, almost touching the floor the entire way. I turn my back to the opposite wall, release air from my lungs and draw up my knees. I look up at the sunshine glimmering off each of my air bubbles as they reach for the undulating surface. It reminds me of childhood.

Coming up from the bottom, I feel the weight of my hair. It is spread evenly from my shoulders, across my back and the ends are drifting in the blue. I can feel Alain's eyes on me. I know he is staying for me. He spent a decade living in the Indian mountains and I know that there lies his true home. France is but a memory for him and belongs only to his past. He is complex and though our bodies meet, our minds somehow do not. Gianni comes over to the poolside, his large browned feet softly drumming the concrete as he walks toward me.

'Why don't you take a swim in the ocean? I need to talk with you. It is important,' he says, glancing to see if Alain is still there.

I sense his tone and lift myself out with arms still strong from years of dancing. Inside, I get a sarong. All the sarongs here are brightly coloured, giving the impression of a place with no problems, an impression we know to be far from the case. I sense as I put on my own sarong that I am about to walk into a problem of my own. My loose leather sandals crunch loudly as they part the smooth pebbles at the front of the villa.

'Get on!'

I like being on the back of his motorcycle. I am relieved that we are not wearing helmets and the warm breeze feels so good as I close my eyes and just inhale the countryside around me. I hold his body close to mine as we sway from side to side, our forward motion dancing with the winding road to the sea. We slow down as we leave the main road and bounce on to the footpath formed in the sand between the reeds.

My bare feet, in the sand now, are soaking up the last of the day's warmth. The sun begins to sink towards the horizon and the waves crash down angrily. We stand for a while looking out. The sky is pink and orange on the horizon but is being swallowed up by an ominous grey that sweeps right over us, ushering in the night. Perhaps it will rain. I like the rain here. It beats down hard as if thrown from the heavens. To be drenched here is to be purified, to feel at one with the earth, to smell the trees and the ground as they should be smelt.

I am aware of the protracted silence we share. Gianni finally speaks.

'Alain is a good man, you know. He is my best friend. He will be good to you.'

'I know this, Gianni.'

He stops me, makes me look at him. I force my head forward again towards the water, staring out to sea. My face is solemn.

'Something happened to you, didn't it? I know you. You are not the same woman who was here three months ago. Who did this to you?'

'Gianni, I'm fine.' I don't want to talk about a thing, remember a thing, about the attack. And besides, that is not the main problem now and I think both of us know it.

Sitting here on the beach together with no one else in sight, it would not surprise me if he suggested we go running naked into the water just for a laugh. It's not that anything would happen. He has thus far been too respectful for that, but there is still something tangible between us that is never spoken of. We have too often shared a bed together but not our bodies. It annoys me that he is bringing the subject down to this, down to 'what happened'. I understand the sentiment. He cares for me. He wants only a good man to be with this woman that he cannot have. I stand up.

'Just give him a chance.' Gianni's voice is subdued by the sound of the ocean tide as I walk back towards the path where we left the bike. Gianni takes my hand in his and squeezes gently.

'You will be all right, *chiquita*.' He presses my body into his and kisses my forehead. Accustomed to speaking Spanish in the villa, he uses the term of endearment with me often. It is one of few words that I understand.

'Let's get back. Maybe we'll go into town and dance a little?'

'Sure.' I say flatly.

I would rather stay at home, open a bottle of wine and talk until three in the morning. I continue to find these men more fascinating the more I know of them. Gianni in particular has a wild and mysterious past. His left-wing politics brought trouble even in his university days but the root runs much deeper. I know this from a mysterious comment he made to me on one of our trips abroad together. He refused to speak of it in detail. I have known him the longest and after spending time with him I discovered I had finally crossed paths with someone who intrigued me in a way I never had been before.

I have known Gianni for a year or so now. We met here in South-East Asia, through a small Italian community in which we had mutual friends. Though I had loved this country always, I had never considered moving before we became close. My mind flits back and forth from the past to the present and I wonder how we all ended up where we are.

He is speeding his way down the narrow pathway towards the road. It is getting dark and though we are not far, we are not properly dressed to be out like this at night. I have no fear. Somehow I trust, instinctively, that I am safe with him though I could not say why I know this with such certainty.

Perhaps he senses my feelings, because we go back to the villa. Pulling up outside, I see Alain in the kitchen already cooking. As I walk in I notice Javier stretched out on the pillows watching some nature documentary. Two lions are mating, and Javier's eyes are fixed on the screen. I make a sound with my teeth like the Afro-Caribbean people do as if to say 'typical'. It is a thing I had learned to do in childhood, a thing that my brother and I learned to do at the same school.

'Brava! Brava!' Gianni sees the television and is drawn in. He grabs a beer from the fridge, still watching, and settles down on another cushion close to Javier.

Alain is waiting for me to approach him. He smiles at me sideways as he cooks and I can see that he has a deep thought in his head. Whether it is to do with me or the cooking I cannot say. I go over to him and kiss him lightly on the cheek, then gently press my soft salty lips against his. He turns and puts his hands behind the small of my back, pulling me close to his own body, feeling the contours of my hips and my belly against him. He presses his lips against mine once more and then releases me and gets back to stirring a pot.

'You will make me burn something. I never burn anything, you know,' he says with pride. Then, 'Did you and Gianni have a good time at the beach?'

'Yes, there was a gorgeous sunset but we didn't get to see it all.'

'Why did Gianni want to talk with you? Is there something wrong?' he says this to me in a low voice; reaching towards me. Could he surely have been oblivious to everything? I wonder to myself momentarily. Then I remember the passion that we shared when I first met him and realise that all really should be right.

'No, no, there was nothing wrong, nothing serious. It's all sorted out now.' I lie with such ease it scares me. 'Do you want some wine?' I ask to change the subject.

'I already opened a bottle,' he grins. His full gaze is on me now and his eyes look as if they are consuming me, taking my body with his very eyes. I blush.

'Don't look like that, *chérie*,' he says. 'You are beautiful. I like you in that sarong. It is so innocent-looking, so light and the wind caresses it as I would caress you. It would be so easy to pick you up in my arms.'

'Thank you,' I say, looking at him with more courage, with the courage of the woman that is still inside me, still dormant but there.

'I have some damn work to catch up on, *mon amour*. I'll be in the room while you finish cooking. I would not want to be the first to ruin your meals!' I laugh as I slowly step backwards.

Alain grabs my wrist and draws me to him. He kisses me again, urging my lips apart, demanding to taste me. His passion takes me unawares and my lips part involuntarily letting him inside my body, feeling the fleeting rush of desire go across my belly. Yes, there is still something there between us. My heart is beating in my chest. Perhaps he can feel it pounding.

'If I was not making dinner . . .' he says, his eyelids lowered, his face close to mine, his eyes fixed on my mouth.

'*Por aquí, no!* Take it to the bedroom!' Gianni laughs, his head still facing the television. We must be reflected in the screen.

My face goes red and I pull back. I hear a low chuckle in Javier's throat too. It makes me feel like a child again. The woman retreats with me towards the bedroom.

I pick up a heavy university textbook, but my mind is still focused on the feeling and desire within me. I am not fully part of this group but it feels as if it's where I belong. I am tired of that pinch in my heart that I feel each day. The culture in this home is a rope around me, drawing me in. Learning about what it is that they all share, their common past is what I know I want. I drop the weight of the text on the futon and it lands with a hard thud. I get out my laptop instead. I need to learn their language, to share their history. The decision forms rapidly.

For the next months of my life I will be living far from here. And though I will miss the boys, I am excited at the prospect. My mind is clear. If I am to gain a sense of belonging amongst these men, I must follow their paths.

I am going to Cuba.

JORDAN TAYLOR

The Woods

THE THINGS THAT HAPPENED to me at boarding school at Barton were too terrible to believe. Every day of those three years, I lived under a thick blanket of fear, one that I only later came out of. I've only surmised its limits with the advantage of years.

One Sunday, all twenty of us – all of us in the school soccer contingent – stood on a hill, stamping in the cold. Behind us, some forty metres away, lay Barton proper. Before us was the vast and untrammelled wilderness: the grounds, primordial under a blanket of fresh snow.

A man who resembled both a monkey and a travel agent stood in front of us. Our coach. Coach Grezin.

'Today is, how do you say? The first day of the new year,' he said, noticing the looks shooting from eye to eye. He grimaced as if something had bitten him.

'Why you still staring? Go. Go. Tomorrow is hardest practice of season,' he shooed us to depart.

And we ran. Beside Grezin, the assistant coach, a chipper white-haired man named Dumont, watched us go off.

Our furred calves traced fairy paths in the snow. Barton, like an island, hemmed in by the Old Man's fence at one end and the long slope down to the highway at the other, bore a wintry alien visage – frosted picnic tables and broken-up hillocks punctuated the landscape and bodies of water transformed into reflective black surfaces.

'There's something beautiful about it,' I ventured.

Just behind, six inches shorter than me, Dan Carson panted heavily. His blond hair sparkled with snow. When he noticed me looking at him he gave a tight smile, and pressing his hand to his heart, he pantomimed an exhausted face.

He hadn't heard.

Those long runs could hypnotise you. With the snow crunching under my feet, I imagined the upcoming student gallery showing: I would sell a painting for fifty thousand dollars. Then I thought how my mother, the art agent, would react. And the world's appreciation of my completely new kind of art, one talked about all over the television, where I would appear explaining, 'I've painted myself out. What I really want to do now is act.'

The showing was on the twenty-sixth. I had already told Dan when it was. When he took in a particular effort, one with water and caves in it, I would explain it to him in a cool, dialectic way: 'You just don't get it. It's got a history.'

In my mind, he teased me, displaying his inspiring, musical laugh.

'A sexual history?' he'd say.

That was the kind of thing I thought about in those days.

*

We stopped on a hill for a thirty-second rest, beside a trash can that looked post-apocalyptic in the snow. The still, very deep lake lay formidably in the distance.

Charlie – tall and typically good-looking – took three quick steps back from the trash can, clearly signalling his intent as he raised his hand clutching a sweet wrapper. The entire team looked on in anticipation. In one swift move, he threw himself backwards and launched the wrapper in a smooth arc. It landed well to the left of the dustbin.

'Shit!'

We set off again. The next ten minutes were pure hell – every hill was steeper than the last. The course was legendary. We ran it once a year.

Dan ran behind me and whispered, 'Run, run, run, run, run, run.'

I went back to imagining the art agent. Warmed by this, I survived. Eventually we swept around in a gentle arc and returned back to Barton.

We entered the school via the ancient Benjamin Mauer foyer, where a statue stood of its namesake. As a dedicated student, I had made a concerted effort to learn the history of the school. The original foyer had burned down in 1882. Only in recent years had it been officially renamed. Though no one could quite remember what the new name was supposed to be, or why the change had even been necessary, someone, at some point, discovered that Ben Mauer – whoever he'd been – had once done something terrible. Yet I couldn't for the life of me remember what it was. In any case, Mr Mauer looked very jolly. He was an old man, patrician in bearing, his right hand pointing down a dark hall to the education building, which on a Sunday was defunct and entirely empty. As I stared at him, I realised that his left hand would have once pointed at nothing. I knew immediately it was a funny realisation, one I had to tell my friends. I wanted them to think I was thoughtful.

Now, it led to the modern addition to the building, that currently funnelled towards us the smell and murmur of a hundred of our peers. And lunch. We were all very hot, still panting from the cold; I could feel the blood in my ears.

'That was the worst,' said Charlie. His hands rested on his knees. Tall and lanky, he often struggled with endurance. I saw the line of freckles running parallel to the bridge of his nose.

I volunteered, 'At least it's chicken fingers today.'

Charlie didn't say anything, so I started, 'I can't believe it's not the two thousands any more.'

I hadn't explicitly mapped it out, but the path was obvious, if vague: from 'Wow, it's already the 2010s,' to 'time passes so fast,' to a comment about how Barton was built over two hundred years ago, to the aggrandising goal of making a humorous aside about the statue's arm.

But they were so hungry they didn't answer. Charlie and Dan started walking towards the cafeteria.

'Did you know this was built before World War Two?'

But they were already gone.

*

Once he'd eaten, Charlie suddenly remembered. 'I can't believe I didn't make that three pointer.' He looked from Dan to me and back.

He honestly believed that nothing worse had ever happened than missing a three pointer. I, of course, knew different. I wanted to shout; ridiculously, right there in the cafeteria, I wanted to shout.

I wanted to say: 'Much worse things have happened. People die every day. Five million people have died in Rwanda. I've seen them! I've seen the flies crawling in their ears. And every executive, wherever he might work, is a dog; all of their work to make money and get oil is ruining this country, no, this planet, and you're not going to live to twenty-five because of global warming.'

What I really wanted was for Charlie to suffer some terrible disaster that would instil him with a crisis of confidence or let him know what it was to feel unworthy. I wanted to see his determination crushed; I wanted him to be humiliated, unable to assert his own opinions. All the girls liked him, and the girls supported, as I saw it, the insufferable ego that made him so rankling to talk to. Nothing could ever convince him that he didn't have the right, say, to talk to a girl, to dream of girls. Even when a girl rejected him, infuriatingly, his response was either to think, 'Ah, that bitch!' or to whine to Dan and me. But he never, ever thought that he'd had no right to approach her or that, in rejecting him, she had been utterly right. He didn't have the perspective to know that he, too, given the chance, might eat shit, or that he could be a woman, or that he could . . . he infuriated me.

Dan rolled his eyes, 'Yeah, dude, you should have made it. These potatoes are awful.'

We ate.

Eventually, as suddenly reminded of the fact by the meal, I said, 'Did you know there's been a famine in India?'

'Was it bad?' Dan asked.

'Pretty bad. I was reading about it yesterday. Some people ate their own shit to survive.'

Charlie's mouth crimped down at one edge. He had a broad, flat mouth. He stabbed at his plate with his fork.

'Are there vitamins in that?'

I shrugged, 'You'll do anything.'

He replied, 'I would never do that.'

'There was this one guy who became a prostitute.' I was speaking off-handedly, paying attention to my food. 'He did it to feed his family.

JORDAN TAYLOR | The Woods   173

It was this really weird article. Apparently, prostitution is illegal there, so they sent him to prison.'

Charlie said, 'So what you're saying is there are gay prostitutes in India?'

I was oddly satisfied: it was as if I'd wanted to shock him in exactly this way, or as if I'd won an argument. I was staring at Charlie, but in my peripheral vision I could see Dan looking back and forth between our faces.

'I guess. I mean the important thing was they had to do something.'

'Hmpph.' I had thought Charlie would bite on that comment.

Then he added, 'Yeah, but the point is those people aren't Americans.'

'Sure.' I raised one thumb on the hand on the table, a quick, upward jerk as if to allow that what he'd said was true.

'You could have been born there,' I said.

'But I wasn't.' There was food in his mouth.

'Well, what if you were?'

He shook his head.

'I wasn't. Besides, there are people in America who are starving. You don't need India. There are bad times in Detroit.'

'Well, sure.'

He said, 'That's why foreign aid is retarded.'

I vaguely felt the need, again, to beat him up, to make him beg, to shake him, to make him feel worthless and see a different perspective. But breaking another's will is impossible and it would have taken far more than I had at my disposal. But all I could say hopelessly was, 'Whatever.' I looked at Dan, who was staring down at his shoes, and felt that the discussion, wherever it had come from, had accomplished its purpose.

We got up, bussed our trays and headed back towards our rooms.

*

As usual for those long Sundays, when we were stressed and ready to kill each other, things devolved into an argument.

'Practice yesterday was so good,' said Charlie.

Dan snorted. 'I don't think so. I hate running.'

It was Charlie's turn to shake his head.

'Do you realise that zone we played last game has never been played before? No team in the state works as hard as we do.'

Dan replied, 'I didn't like it.'

Charlie narrowed his eyes, examining Dan's pupils as if he suspected an impurity. 'You just don't want to work hard.'

'Maybe.'

Charlie caught my gaze and shook his head, as if to say, 'Why does he even play?'

I gave him my look: hand out apologetically, eyebrows raised, mouth shunted to one side in sympathy, a defensive little smile. It was the same expression I used when someone caught me unprepared by looking at me during class, or when someone caught my eye across the room at a party. A look that said, 'Well, here we are,' or 'What are you gonna do about it?', a look that begged, 'Don't see anything other than this.' Sometimes when Dan and I caught each other's eye in physics, we grimaced, or I double-bounced my eyebrows at him.

He smirked.

Charlie said definitively, 'Fine. You're gonna be a mediocre player.'

And with that he changed the subject, 'Are you coming to Ann's party? You have to. You didn't come to the last one. If you don't, I'll only be there with Claire. And Ann really wants to talk to you.'

We stopped. We'd reached the door to Dan's room. He was going to take a shower. We paused outside.

'She wants to hook up with you,' Charlie explained.

'Did they get the Corona?' asked Dan.

'They bought so much alcohol.'

'Hendricks?'

Charlie nodded.

'Fuck,' said Dan, appreciatively, signalling his desire to go, whatever excuses he'd marshalled and had ready. A hot flush washed into my face – at their easy reconciliation, at how little the previous argument seemed to matter now that a party had come under discussion.

'You have to come,' Charlie looked sideways at Dan, 'because you lied to me last time.'

'I'll come.'

I stood at the door, listening to them.

Dan was about to go inside.

'See you guys later.'

'What are you doing later?' I asked Dan.

I had a physics study session, held by a Barton teacher every Sunday. Charlie would walk with me part of the way, because his room was in the same direction.

He laughed, 'Actually I'm going to get a stick. Me and Kate and Tiana need to make a model of the life cycle for bio, and I need to build a model of a deer.'

*

Charlie and I walked on. I always felt awkward when I was alone with Charlie. I could tell that he liked me, but I couldn't tell how to react to him. He had an entire vocabulary of mini, masculine gestures that made me uncomfortable. Part of the issue – though not the main part – among the three of us was that Dan was always on the edge of forgiving Charlie, while I knew that I could never really like him. I always worried their connection was going to squeeze me out.

'Dan's such a little kid.' It was so clearly the beginning of a rant about Dan's immaturity that I didn't need any time to sniff it out. Yet I folded immediately.

'I mean, that's true,' I hazarded, laughing. I wanted him to see that I agreed. 'I mean, I see what he's saying a little. But today wasn't even that tiring.'

'Yeah.'

'Is that party the same one Nancy's gonna be at?' I asked.

His brow knitted. 'I think so.'

I nodded.

'Do you talk to her a lot?' he asked.

'Yeah . . .' I thought teasing was forthcoming, but he said nothing.

I had actually known Charlie longer than Dan. We'd been friends since our first day at Barton, and I met Dan six months later. Dan met Charlie first, was soccer buddies first with him, and was now, more privately, friends with me. We both liked the woods.

Charlie and I discussed our assignments. He clutched his books to his chest. There was something both playful and uncompromising about him when he was alone with me; he always looked me straight in the eye and he occasionally devised some test that I always failed to pass. One time he said, 'We've known each other for two years now. I love you,' and I laughed, nervous. I had never said that to anyone but my parents. He meant it with some valence that completely eluded me. Another time he walked in front of me and put himself in a position to block me as I walked down the hallway. I knew it was some game. I dodged left, then right. He wouldn't let me past. He watched the fear grow in my eyes. Finally, he relented, chuckling, and pushed me towards the classroom.

We reached my classroom. Charlie walked on alone. I realised, suddenly, that my heart was beating quickly. I was nervous, or exhilarated. I couldn't tell when this new state had come upon me, but it was definitely there. As the tutor, a droning Barton English specimen named Dana Blitz, started class, I discovered I felt wonderful. The image of Dan and Charlie's arguing replayed itself over and over in my head. I found that, somehow, this new emotion had come mysteriously from that. Something I cared about quite a lot had been exchanged or discussed during Dan's attempt to resist Charlie. The clear endpoint for the new emotion seemed to be to talk to Dan; I was excited at the prospect.

I texted him under the desk.

In a few seconds, my phone buzzed.

Finally, I summoned the courage to bring up the party: 'Still going to get that stick tonight?'

'Sure, dude. You want to come along?'

'Yeah, I haven't really been able to fall asleep lately anyway . . .' I replied.

What I was hoping for was a 'Why?' back, which would lead to a whole dialogue that might eventually go straight to the heart of things, a reply from him, as if finally understanding: 'Sam, I think you're being mysterious. Is something wrong?' I always imagined a person, at the beginning of a new class, who would not only be extraordinarily good-looking but would realise that I felt I was acting in a significant way with everyone, a person who would approach me after class and save me, 'you're drowning.' When that person didn't show up, I would attempt to manipulate what everyone thought of me, controlling my expressions so that when the teacher looked away I nodded, so that they could see I was casual and basically uncaring.

The last time I'd gone out to party with Dan, I'd imagined that drinking would facilitate, somehow, a greater connection, in which we lay in sleeping bags in the dark. He would say, 'I just get really scared sometimes,' and so we would both feel some greater connection sparking between us.

But instead he said 'Me neither! You should come! Tiana and Kate are coming.' I felt drained, suddenly, at seeing the names of the two girls, the chipperness of the 'You should come.' But I realised that I simply wanted to interact with someone and not to be alone with myself; I needed to have something to do. So I said, 'When?'

AMANDA COWLEY

The Granddaughter Clock

1

HE DIED AT SIX-THIRTY on the evening of Wednesday, 25 April 1990, at a rest home in Beechmont, Australia. He was eighty-three years old.

During his lifetime he had imagined a thousand ways in which he might die, from a broken heart to an exploding bomb, a car crash, a drowning, and even murder at the hands of his second wife. But it had all been a waste of energy as he was to die from the most common killer of man – the heart attack.

He was not alone in dying on that day. Dexter Gordon, the jazz saxophonist, died of kidney failure at the age of sixty-seven in Philadelphia, and tens of thousands of others died on Planet Earth, although he knew none of them.

Earlier that morning he had observed the room in which he had been living for the past few months. He considered it rather nondescript, and he was right. A square pale pink box contained: a chest of drawers upon which a rather tired bunch of flowers drooped in a vase, a small slim pine wardrobe, a side table and a single bed, all of which sat on a beige vinyl-tiled floor. The walls were bare, as he had asked for the seascape painting to be taken down, and his personal belongings were limited to a few books and a small brown leather suitcase, filled with writings and clippings from the war, which remained under the bed. In front of the veranda doors stood a short, round formica table sporting a box of man-size tissues, a glass of water and a Bible. An upright chair with pink upholstery sat on one side of the table and opposite there was a dated, but exceptionally comfortable, floral chair.

It was from this floral chair that he continued his favourite pastime of bird watching, sitting for hours while rainbow lorikeets flirted in the trees, ducking and diving between the branches of the rough-barked eucalyptus with its silver-blue leaves. The macaw, a large white bird with a plumed head, was a beauty until it opened its beak and let out a rasping screech.

He had grinned as he remembered the day one of the residents played a piece of Paganini on his violin, no doubt showing off to attract the attention of the female residents. Within seconds a macaw plum-meted from the roof on to the patio below having screeched its last breath. For Jonathan it had provided perfect ammunition for weeks against that particular old codger.

Being an Englishman, he had insisted on his tea being presented in a very precise way from the day after he had arrived. Having been offered what he considered 'cat's piss', he had told the orderly to 'Go and get a decent cuppa.' The nurses and orderlies were under strict instruction to adhere to his whims as he had paid an extra premium for special attention. The pot must therefore be china and not metal, and the tea was to be left to brew for four minutes exactly. He insisted that the milk was 'fresh, mind, not those awful tiny, long-life plastic con-tainers which are impossible to open for anyone with adult fingers. And make sure you put it in a small jug.'

He had scored low on the nurses' and orderlies' invisible star chart which graded the residents' behaviour, a way to lighten what at times was tedious work. When a resident was as pompous and cantankerous as he was, they would refer to him, behind his back, as 'Mr Zero Stars.'

'Good afternoon Mr Walker, I'm Sister Constance. Would you like a chat?'

'Yes . . . yes, I would, do come in.' He did not want to appear too eager, but having chosen Beechmont because it was affiliated with St Joseph's convent, he was relieved to have a visitor at last.

Sister Constance was in her early fifties. A large cross on a cord – such as a bishop would wear – hung around her neck. It was the first thing he had noticed about her, the second being her blue iridescent eyes which sparkled. Wearing the regulation black habit, her hair was covered in a black headdress with a band of white framing her face. She was a slim woman, who obviously took care of herself, both physically and mentally. She was strong, with a ruddy complexion bearing the signs of a life out of doors – he imagined her trekking through the bush on her days off, sporting a pair of walking boots and a wide-brimmed hat. She was equally fit mentally, and certainly a disciplined person – because, first, what nun isn't? Second, her conversation was always brimming over with biblical exegesis.

Although Jonathan had long ago abandoned hermeneutics and theorising for *The Times* crossword puzzle, and more recently, the *Beechmont Weekly Gazette*, he waited most eagerly for her visits and their lively debates. Sister Constance radiated integrity, from the way she held herself to her conversation. Finding this deeply appealing, he recognised it as something he lacked or as something he had lost.

She talked in a once-familiar language about religion – a language that he had spoken fluently, but now, in his twilight years, had lost. In front of the residents, he had become belligerent and even a little abusive to the point of shocking himself. At night, alone, he wondered if he should be muzzled like one of those beastly dogs in the park whose owners are avoiding a law suit. But when he sat with Sister Constance he mellowed. They enjoyed numerous debates and conversations about his struggle with faith. He admired her straightforward approach, never pussyfooting around him because he was elderly. She was prepared to bat to and fro big theological questions. After one hour of weighty discussion she would leave as promptly as she had arrived, never staying longer, even when he tried to bribe her with a cup of tea. 'I have other people to see, Jonathan, but we shall meet again next week. Until then may the Lord bless you and keep you.'

'Yes, and may his face shine upon me too, Sister,' he would add, with a mark of sarcasm.

'I prayed for you last night, Jonathan,' said Sister Constance when she arrived at her usual time on the day before his death.

The sun showed itself from behind a cloud and blazoned through the veranda doors, welcoming her into the room.

'That was a waste of time,' he had replied.

Arriving with her usual promptness she greeted him by taking hold of his hand and giving it a gentle squeeze, after which she sat down in the less comfortable wooden chair, and did something she had not done before. From a hidden pocket in her habit she took a tiny unmarked bottle of lavender oil which she uncapped and from which she proceeded to pour just a few drops on to his palm. It was absorbed almost immediately: thirsty as a desert is for rain. She then looked straight into his eyes and replied, 'Prayer is hardly a waste of my time, Jonathan. I felt the Lord say to me that you need to return to your first love.'

'My first love?' he replied. The words hit him like an incendiary bomb. He shivered and then smiled.

'My goodness, Jonathan, that provoked a response, you went quite peculiar. What are you smiling at?' she said.

'My first love.'

'What does it mean to you?' she said, knowing full well that she had struck a chord.

'When yet I had not walked above a mile, or two, from my first love, and looking back at that short space, could see a glimpse of his bright face.'

He took a long, deep breath.

'That's lovely, Jonathan. Isn't it by Henry Vaughan?'

'Yes, it is. It's called "The Retreat" . . . I learnt it by heart as a young boy.'

'So Jesus was your first love? The invisible God made visible,' she said.

'Yes . . . he was. But I lost him, you see. He faded from my life and now I can't respect a deathbed conversion.'

'Better on a deathbed than not at all,' she said, 'but we are not talking about conversion. I'm talking about you returning to the faith of your youth, before the difficulties of life overwhelmed you.'

'Happy those early days! When I shined in my angel-infancy,' he replied. 'It's not that simple, Sister.'

'Does it have to be so hard?' she said.

'I can't forgive God for what happened.'

'What did happen? You've never really told me.'

He lowered his head. 'I have spent many years trying to forget.'

'Has it worked?' she replied.

'Has what worked?'

'Have you forgotten?'

'You know I haven't.'

They both fell silent. She knew that if she spoke he might shut down again as he had done on other visits. She also knew, from her training, that she was there to listen. Listening was one of the ways she had learned to love.

'Why do you think he allows children to die? Is it his plan? If he is such a big God why doesn't he stop the killing?' he said.

'Who was killed, Jonathan?'

He sat, suspended in time, concerned that in speaking the words he might betray the memory of someone not spoken of for over seventy years.

'My sister.'

2

In 1913, the Walkers lived on Ambleside Drive in Southend, in a semi-detached Victorian house with two bay windows. It was not a house of great character or great charm, but it was home to Jonathan, aged five, and his four older siblings.

Doris was adored by all her brothers – not because she was the only girl but because she was the kindest person they knew. Being thirteen and the eldest, she held some kudos with her parents, especially Father, of whom they were all a little frightened: a tall, thin, draconian man, Victorian in manner, issuing orders on a daily basis; a fierce advocate of abstinence from any form of liquor, the brandy bottle in the medicine chest having never, as far as anyone knew, been touched.

When Father shouted at her naughty brothers Doris would mediate, reaching across the table, her delicate fingers touching his hand, 'Don't worry yourself, Pa. You mustn't let them annoy you.' Her words soothed him like a lullaby.

The pebbles were solid and painful beneath the young boy's feet, the cold wind and frothy waves smarting the backs of his legs. 'Come here, my little man,' shouted his sister as she chased him round and round; her blonde ringlets springing up and down on her chest.

'No . . . stop it . . . stop it!' Jonathan screamed with delight as Doris tickled him until he was almost sick.

Doris was elevated in five-year-old Jonathan's eyes simply because she was affectionate, a quality which was more than wanting in Mother. When he came down to breakfast one morning, having dressed himself for the first time, his brothers laughed at him and pointed at the buttons of his cardigan wrongly matched with the buttonholes. Doris, meanwhile, put them right and then lifted him on to her lap, her sweet breath filling his ear as she whispered, 'Don't listen to them. You are my favourite little man.'

Doris lay in bed. She cried out in pain. A doctor arrived but due to his misdiagnosis, appendicitis soon developed into peritonitis. A few days later another doctor and a nurse arrived at the house and busied themselves in the room upstairs while the family crowded around the kitchen range with its red-hot iron openings. Jonathan's eldest brother Wilf, who had just turned twelve, roasted chestnuts with the iron tongs whilst Harry and Eddy, known as the *rascals* by Mother, kept themselves busy by making paper aeroplanes.

Father and Mother left the room from time to time to go to Doris. When they came back they asked favours of the children in an attempt to hide their anguish. 'Will you warm this pillow for me?' or 'Could you put the kettle on for tea?'

Jonathan sneaked upstairs to see what was happening. Putting his ear to his sister's bedroom door he strained to listen. The door was soon opened by a nurse carrying a bedpan to the bathroom, bustling past him, 'Out of the way,' she said.

And so he ran to the bedroom he shared with his three brothers and fell on his knees beside the bed, saying, 'Please God, don't let Doris die. Please God, don't let Doris die.'

But that night, death came to Ambleside Drive. It swooped down and stole Doris.

In the morning, while his brothers slept, he got up and dressed in his school trousers, shirt and jumper. Running downstairs to the breakfast room he saw his father standing with his back to the door.

'There will be no school today, Jonathan. I don't want to hear a word out of you. Go to your room.' he said, without turning round.

Peering around his father's long legs he saw his mother's slight frame in a heap on the floor. She was crying and muttering into her handkerchief, next to the fire that had well and truly gone out.

The boy bolted upstairs back to Wilf. 'She's dead,' he shouted.

'I know, little man. I know.' Wilf said, enfolding his sibling in his arms as he burst into tears.

Why, God? Why did you not answer my prayer? Where were you?

Throughout the day people came and went from the house. The boys were told to stay in the bedroom where they played dominoes over and over again until lunchtime when a neighbour came to collect them and walked with them to the park.

That night, as Jonathan lay in his bed, hardly breathing, he heard his mother wailing downstairs. Crying, he retreated down under his sheets where it was dark and private. After a short time he found it hard to breathe and surfaced to a room in darkness. Hearing Wilf's deep breathing in the bed next to him, he cried out, 'Doris?'

Nothing happened.

He heard Wilf next to him sigh deeply. Turning over he took his small, well-worn teddy, snuggled it up to his mouth and began sucking his thumb, whimpering as he fell asleep.

The next morning a coffin arrived and was placed on the extended table in the dining room, next to a large aspidistra. The room was filled with highly polished, dark wood furniture and chairs that were still in their protective coverings.

Doris was placed in the coffin and the curtains were closed. A few close neighbours who had been invited to view her came with small posies to place on her body. Jonathan was considered too young to look at his sister and so when the women were in the dining room having tea with his mother he crept into the room. Climbing up on a chair, he lifted the heavy lid of the box. Peering in, he saw his sister, like a large porcelain doll, in her best cream dress, with bright-coloured flowers tied with raffia on her chest and in her hands. As he reached out to touch her, the lid fell suddenly with a loud bang that stirred the family in the next room.

Mother dashed in. 'Jonathan, come away from there. What do you think you are doing?' She put her hands over his eyes and pushed him out of the room.

On the day of the funeral the three older boys went with their parents in the hearse from the house. As he left the house, Father said to Jonathan, 'Do as your aunt tells you. Be a good boy.'

Jonathan helped lay the table, the table that Doris had just vacated, trotting behind his aunt as she placed a pile of plates down. He then laid out white napkins, all the while his aunt solemnly singing about the better land, the pearly gates and the joys of heaven.

Finally, the family arrived back, followed by two doctors and the minister, friends, relations, teachers and schoolgirls, all dressed in black. Blackness and sorrow permeated the house just as smoke billows into a room when the flue is blocked. Mother had not really recovered and the little patience Father had was no longer in evidence.

Jonathan was taken to the grave before the flowers wilted and as he stood on the mound of earth he imagined Doris in her dress, just as he had seen her, asleep in her coffin, waiting to get her wings – believing that maybe Doris had not been a girl at all, but rather an angel whom God had called back to heaven.

One afternoon when Mother had left the house, Wilf gathered the brothers together in the dining room and read aloud the many letters of condolence that had poured through the letterbox.

'We are devastated to hear of Doris's passing and trust that the good Lord has taken her into heaven. She was such an angel and we hope you will find some comfort in knowing she is no longer in pain.'

'Read another one.' said Harry, Eddy and Jonathan, in unison.

'Doris was such a dear child. We can only imagine that the Lord had a purpose for her in heaven.'

'You see, boys, she is in heaven with the angels,' said Wilf.

All of them nodded, eagerly wanting a life for their sister that surpassed the grave.

'Will we see her again?' asked Harry.

'I believe it with all my heart.'

Jonathan, rubbing his tummy, cried out, 'I miss her so much, it hurts . . .'

MADELINE PARSONS

One of Ireland's Happy Families

O N THE NIGHT of the performance, Mrs Doherty gives Liam a gentle shove and he rushes on to the stage in his wolf costume. 'Aughhh!' he roars. He can hear the parents laughing and whispering to each other, but he knows not to look into the audience – actors must never do that, Mrs Doherty had told them. And anyway, why would he want to look into the audience? It would be a miracle if his mam turned up. Don't think about her, he tells himself, think about being a wolf. He curls his hands into claws, imagining his fur standing on end, with sharp nails primed, his mouth crammed full of brutal teeth.

'Aughhh!' he roars again. The rest of the boys, dressed as sheep pretending to munch grass, scatter when they see him. Joseph – he's the Boy – cries 'Wolf, Wolf,' and runs wildly around the stage. Liam dives on to Kevin and worries him to the ground where he lies. Dead. He leaps on to Owen next, showing him his teeth, his long red tongue. 'Aughhhhhh! You dumb sheep. You're claimed.' He digs his claws into Owen's back and gives an extra fierce roar as he pins him down. He's not supposed to, but sheep starts to wrestle wolf. Liam gets him in a headlock. From the audience comes a great gust of laughing and clapping, and some encouraging yells: 'Come on the sheep!'

Inside his wolf costume, Liam feels sweat trickle down his back, gathering around the elastic in his underpants. It's all wrong, he thinks. Sheep are not supposed to fight back like that. So he sums up all his strength and forces Owen on to his back, kneeling on his chest. Owen's crying now, hard, tears and snot getting mixed into his sheep costume. I don't care, Liam thinks. *I'm* the wolf! He puts his hands around

Owen's throat and squeezes, but the sheep continues to struggle under him, his face red and determined. From the corner of his eye Liam sees a man jump up from his seat and hurtle towards him; others in the audience are standing up, pointing and screaming at the stage. He can hear Mrs Doherty shouting, 'Freeze, Liam, freeze!' He knows that's the command to STOP, but her words are drowned out by a voice that rolls up from his belly and explodes from his mouth. It says: 'If yeh don't shut up, yeh fucken' bitch, I'll fucken' kill yeh.'

*

Two days earlier, Mrs Doherty had asked Liam to stay back after school; she had something important to ask him, she said. She perched on a desk opposite him, and peeled the wrapper off a packet of Polo mints.

'Take two,' she said, 'one for each cheek.'

Mrs Doherty popped a mint into her mouth, sucked on it, and smiled at him. She must be as old as his mam, he thought, very old anyway, with lines around her mouth and eyes. It puzzled him that she didn't have grey hair but, after some thought, he decided that she must use the stuff they advertise on the telly that makes your hair go all red and shiny. It makes you feel young enough to walk into a shop and buy a pair of high-heeled shoes.

'So, Liam,' she said, 'how are things?'

'Fine.'

'How's your mam?'

People were always asking him that.

'Fine.'

'It's just that . . . I don't see her coming to school to pick you up these days at all. I was wondering if everything was all right at home?'

He didn't want to look straight at her. She was like one of the saints in those holy pictures they had hanging up in the classroom – she could see into your soul, maybe.

'Everything's grand. Honest.'

He let one of the polo mints rest on his tongue, and then sucked it gently. He could make it last for ages. He always used to beat Marcella, his older sister, in their sucking competitions. He missed Marcella. For months, little by little, she'd snuck all her stuff out of the house, and then, one day, she just never came back.

'And how's Marcella?'

'She's grand. She works in John Frederick's in town – a *salon*. That's French for hairdressing shop.'

'Indeed it is, Liam,' Mrs Doherty said. 'You're great altogether to know things like that. Is she enjoying it?'

'Yeah, she loves it. She'll have her own salon in no time, she said.'

'That's brilliant, Liam,' Mrs Doherty beamed, 'it's great for her to get a job with prospects in these hard times. Your mammy must be glad of the extra money coming in.'

'Yeah, she is.'

'And your brothers will be home for the holidays, too, I expect? It's terrible that we're still exporting our young men to England to dig their roads and build their office blocks. Your mammy will be glad to see them.'

'Yeah, she will.'

Outside, he could hear the lads playing football in the yard before going home. He hoped she'd stop talking soon, so he could get out there too.

Mrs Doherty took off her concerned face and smiled at him.

'You know, Liam, I've been impressed by the work you've been doing in drama club. Really, I have.' She clapped her hands and laughed. 'Don't look so confused. I truly think you have a talent for the stage, young man.'

Wow, Liam thought. Maybe he could be an actor, like Colin Farrell, or Saoirse Ronan. They're from Dublin too.

'So,' she went on, 'you know we're doing *The Boy who cried Wolf* in a couple of days? Well, Joseph Scally has come down with the flu, so I was wondering if you would like to take his place?'

She placed a hand on his arm. Her touch was soft, gentle.

'Perhaps you think you're too old to take part in this sort of play, but . . .' her usual kindly look came over her face '. . . as you are quite small for your age, Liam, you'll easily fit into the Wolf costume. And because you're nine . . .'

'Nine and a half,' he told her.

'. . . I can trust you to do a good job at such short notice. You won't have to learn any lines. You just need to look fierce, and scare the sheep. You'll be brilliant at it.'

She beamed at him. 'Well,' she said, 'what do you think?'

Saying no to Mrs Doherty was like instructing the rain to stop falling.

'Okay,' he said, 'yeah, I can do that.'

It was just a short walk home from school. It took him down the long road towards the Dublin mountains, and then past the stand of dilapidated-looking shops built in the 1960s when the Dublin Corporation, as a sort of afterthought, threw up a few amenities to serve the residents of the recently completed housing estate. He wandered into the local Spar and meandered through the aisles, thinking about what to get for tea. There were mirrors everywhere, so staff could observe small, spindly legged boys in grimy green fleeces like him. But it was not his intention to shoplift that day. He studied the special offers with fierce concentration. Sausages, he decided: buy one, get one free. He had one euro left from the money Marcella had given him the last time he had visited her.

Back at home, he set to cooking tea. First, you light the gas. If there's no gas, you have to put money in the meter. If you've no money, then it's bread and jam for tea, or cornflakes, maybe, but tonight there's gas. And sausages. You have to be careful when you cook sausages. You put a little oil in the pan, let it warm up, but not too much, and then you put in the sausages. You mustn't stab them with a fork before you put them in, because that makes them burst. Marcella taught him that. She taught him most things he knew. Then you stand there and watch them splutter and spatter in the pan. They look like tiny little baby piggies. Aghh, they go, help, I'm burning, someone rescue me, aghh!! But you just turn them over. No, you evil little pigs, you tell them, you have done terrible deeds, you must burn in the fire until you die. They squirm and spit, but you leave them there until they are nice and brown, and cooked all the way through.

His mam didn't fancy sausages that night. They had run out of chips, so it was just sausages. She sat at the Formica table in the kitchen with a brooding look on her face, smoking, while Liam sat opposite her and chewed quietly. She was nothing like Mrs Doherty. His mam's hair was long and brown, with grey bits in it and she always tied it back with an elastic band. She should get some of that hair dye stuff, Liam thought, not red though. That would clash with her purple cheeks.

He told her what Mrs Doherty had said about his being a good actor, and about being picked to be the wolf because Joe Scally had the flu. She raised her cigarette to her lips with a shaking hand and had a long drag. She rested her elbow on the table and stared at him through the smoke.

'Did Mrs Doherty ask any questions about the family?'

'No.'

'Good. Make sure you say nothing to that aul wan about what goes on in this house.'

'She just asked me if I would like to be the Wolf. We're doing it in two days' time.'

'I hope she doesn't expect me to pay for a wolf costume,' she said. 'If she thinks I have money for that sort of shite, she has another think coming.'

The cigarette had nearly burned down to her fingers. She dipped the butt into her glass of water to quench it, then picked up a sausage from her plate and bit into it.

'And I'm fucken sick of eatin' sausages,' she said.

Liam said nothing. Marcella always told him never to answer back. 'Whatever that aul bitch says,' she dinned into him, 'remember never to answer back, never. You save yourself a lot of aggro that way.'

Marcella sometimes called their mam The Wicked Witch of the West – of Dublin! Liam laughed his head off when she came up with that one. It wasn't so funny now that she had left home and moved into a bedsit on the South Circular with her boyfriend, Stefan. Liam would visit them sometimes, on a Sunday. The three of them would have fish and chips and lemonade for their dinner, and Marcella would always give him a few euros for his bus fare home, and to keep him going through the week.

He could hear next door's television, and the kids crying. It must be their bedtime, he thought. They always bawled at bedtime.

His mam lit another cigarette. It took three goes with the matches to light it. She took a huge drag, and blew it out with a sigh. Through the smoke, she devoured him with her eyes, as if she was seeing him for the first time.

'Why, in the name of God, did I ever have children?' she said. 'What possessed me, eh?'

She pointed at the cupboard that squatted in the corner of their dingy kitchen.

'Only for I have the bloody birth certificates, no one would ever know I had two grown-up sons in England, Manchester, or Leeds, or wherever it is, earning good money, while we're struggling back here. It would never occur to them to think of their mother, to send her a few bob now and then. Would it cost them so much even to send a birthday card, for Jaysus' sake? Put a few bob in it? Mean bloody scuts!'

Liam's brothers had been born so long before him that he only vaguely remembered having brothers at all. There was a photograph of them on the kitchen press, though, that he liked to take down and look at occasionally. He would examine minutely every feature of the little group staring out at him from the plastic frame on which was inscribed *Souvenir of Bray*. This was his family, before he had been born, at the seaside. The baby – that's Danno, he would whisper to himself – is in his mam's arms. The other one, Gary, is sitting on his dad's knee. Liam sometimes wondered what it must have been like, to sit on his dad's knee, on a sunny afternoon at the seaside. They're all smiling, sprawled there on the towel, buckets and spades in front of them in the sand. There's a duffel bag next to his dad, probably full of sandwiches and crisps and biscuits, that they would lash into as soon as they finished having their photograph taken. The sun is shining on his mam's smiling face, her red lips, her shiny brown hair, her sunburnt arms. She looks happy. They all do. If you saw that picture in the *Evening Herald*, there would be a headline above it saying: One of Ireland's Happy Families Enjoying a Day Out at the Seaside.

His mam rooted in the shopping bag at her feet, took out a half bottle of Powers, unscrewed the lid and had a swig.

'And there's Marcella,' she said, 'who could be a bit of help to me, only she's fecked off with that bloody Romanian fella she's known for two seconds.'

He's Polish, Liam wanted to correct her, but he didn't say anything.

'Do *you* know where she's living now?' she asked him.

'No, Mam.'

She banged the table so hard the plates rattled.

'Yes, yeh do, yeh lyin' little toe-rag.'

'No, Mam. Honest to God, I don't.'

She stood up, went over to the tap, rinsed her glass, then filled it with what was left of the Powers and sat down again. Her face looked like the black clouds that bump on top of the Dublin mountains just before it starts lashing down with rain.

'You'd think I'd learn, wouldn't yeh?' she said. 'But no!' Her voice sounded as if she wanted to destroy the world. 'For three years I had a bit of peace and quiet in the house after your father fecked off to England that time. Marcella was nearly reared, I got a job cleaning offices at night, made a few bob.' She glowered across the table at Liam. 'But then, what did I go and do? I let your father, the man who could drink the Liffey dry, back into the house. Swore he'd never let me down again, as God was his witness.' She took a large swallow of her drink. 'And guess what?'

'What?'

'I believed him. Would you credit that? And then . . .' she laughed so hard she started to choke. She spluttered to a stop, and stared at him again.

Liam wanted to go, but was afraid if he made a run for it, that would start up the volcano, and if she erupted he was a goner.

'And then,' she said, 'guess what Santy brought me for Christmas?' She didn't wait for a reply. 'YOU!' she roared. 'We called you Liam, after him. But here's the best bit. Six months after your da welcomed you into the world, he went out for a packet of fags and never came back. Would you credit that now? Just fecked off and left me holding the baby.'

He scrunched down into his seat, but she leant across the table towards him. 'You were one massive mistake! Did you know that?'

Flecks of her spittle pattered on to his cheek. He willed his hands not to reach up and wipe them away. She slammed her hand on the table.

'Answer me.'

'Yes, Mam.'

'What were yeh?

'A mistake, Mam.'

'Too fucken' right you were,' she said. She leant back in her chair, and surveyed him. 'But yiz were all mistakes. I wish I never had a single one a yiz.'

She stubbed out her cigarette on the sausages.

'I could've had a life, only for you fucken' kids,' she said. She drained her glass. There was nothing left in the bottle.

It was getting dark. The kids next door had stopped crying. His mam sat opposite him, spent, her head slumped on her chest. All Liam could hear was her breathing and the black clock ticking next to the photograph on the kitchen press.

It was safe to go to his bedroom now, but he stayed at the kitchen table, hating her.

He looked out at the dark clouds, a misty moon appearing occasionally behind them. If only he were a wizard, able to command forces to do as he bade, he could destroy the wicked witch sitting opposite him. He *could* destroy her, he thought, he could. All he had to do was summon the magical powers of the universe. He stared at the moon dipping behind clouds, and raised his arms. Come, he whispered, come. He stretched his fingers into long feelers until he felt as if he could touch the sky itself. Suddenly he felt energy whooshing through his hands and down into his body. He could feel power, and fire, and heat in his head, his belly, his legs. His mam sat opposite him, a dark figure in the gloomy kitchen, snoring, her head thrown backwards now, her throat glowing whitely in the moonlight from the window. He positioned himself opposite her and concentrated hard. Then he pointed at the battered cupboard in the corner of the kitchen, and commanded all the kitchen drawers to open. He willed the knives out of their compartments, every single one of them, and sent them, sharp and speeding, towards her head, her heart, her throat.

LAURENCE JONES

Two Against One

THE VOICES WERE DISTANT at first but familiar. Lucky tried to follow them in the darkness. He looked all around him, tried to figure out which way was up or down, but there was nothing to see, only a solid and impenetrable blackness. He thought he heard his name being called, then a whispering between a man and a woman – but could not be sure. He stretched an arm out in front of him, reached for a surface to frame the space, but there were no walls, no floor, and no memories of how he had arrived there. He was weightless and drifting inside an empty void.

The voices continued to chatter, louder and closer than they had been before. Lucky listened to their grating rhythms, the rumbling baritone of the man's voice overlapped by the sibilant whispers of the woman, a hateful hissing sound which echoed in the emptiness then closed in around him, wrapping itself around his weary body. He began to panic, his thoughts overwhelmed with memories of demons, their red eyes burning as they hunted him down. He tried to gather his senses, reconnect with his body, as the woman's voice constricted and squeezed the air from his lungs.

He thought about the world he had left behind, a cheap motel room on the wrong side of town. He flexed his fingers and toes and, each time he did, lightning flashes sliced through the darkness, images of people and places he loved. The images grew slower and brighter until eventually a familiar numbness flowed through his lower back. He tasted the dryness in his mouth, felt the sunken mattress beneath him and the sweat-soaked sheets on his skin, and knew he had escaped.

'Lucky,' said the man, 'Wake up.'

Lucky lay perfectly still, too scared to open his eyes. The voice was real and it was inside the motel room with him. He tried to place it, then remembered that the boy and girl were still asleep on the other bed. He opened his eyes and scrambled towards them, crashing over the bedside cabinet and falling to the floor, a table lamp shattering in front of him. He dragged himself up the side of their bed and his heart sank as he grasped at nothing but empty sheets.

'Lucky,' said the woman.

Lucky recognised her southern drawl, a siren call he was powerless to resist. He twisted himself around and sat cross-legged on the floor among the broken glass of the lampshade. He looked across the half-lit motel room. Thin shards of sunlight crept inside through the broken blinds, illuminating the dusty surfaces and tired furnishings.

Scott and Emma Barnes were standing by the door. Scott was tall and blond; he was wearing an expensive suit with polished black shoes. Emma stood next to him in dark jeans and a tee-shirt with a band logo on it, her long red hair pulled back in a ponytail. She looked as beautiful as ever but there was a quiet anger in her eyes. She crossed her arms against her chest and shook her head at Lucky.

He scanned the rest of the room and eventually saw the children sitting nervously together on a purple couch by the television. His daughter was staring at the floor, avoiding his gaze, but the boy was looking back at him with expectant eyes, willing him to speak and explain what was happening.

'There you are,' said Lucky. He forced a smile. The boy just shook his head and looked away. Lucky sensed his disappointment, felt another part of their relationship crumbling to dust. He turned to face Scott and Emma.

'How did you find me?' he said.

'Are you kidding me?' said Scott, 'you called us last night, sounded halfway out of your goddamn mind. You don't remember that?'

Lucky shook his head.

'Jesus Christ, Lucky, you scared the crap out me, talking about ghosts and monsters, how something evil was chasing you down. You must remember something?'

Lucky tried to think back. He remembered stealing the phone book from the kiosk and being sick in the parking lot but he had no idea what else had happened, or how long he had been unconscious in the room. He rubbed his hand against his forehead.

'I don't,' he said, 'but I'm sorry. I'm sorry I called you. Things are in a bad way. I'm in a bad way.'

'What's going on, Lucky?' said Scott.

Lucky leaned his head back against the bed and closed his eyes.

'I'll tell you what's going on,' Emma walked up to Lucky and poked a finger at his face. 'He's wasted. He's always wasted. It's what he does best.'

'Enough.' Scott glanced over at the children then turned to Lucky and gave him a reassuring smile. 'You have to tell us what's happened. You wanted us here. You called us for help. You understand that, right?'

Lucky wondered what he had done to deserve such friendship. He hung his head against his chest and tried think where to begin, and when he looked back up, they were all staring at him, even the children. He took a deep breath and exhaled, accepting at last that no one else could help him but himself.

He talked them cautiously through the last three months, as though he could barely believe what had happened himself: the car crash, the broken heart, the drink and drugs, a nightmare that began with a letter in a book.

'I wish to God I'd never found it,' he said. 'Turns out she'd left me anyway long before she died. She meant everything, Scott. Guess the goddamn joke's on me.'

'You don't know for sure she was having an affair,' said Scott.

'Believe me . . . I know.'

He told them about the Raven and the nights of partying, how just as he thought he had left the past behind, he had begun to see things, terrible things, his dead wife and wild dogs and demons, and that now something malevolent was pursuing him, hunting and haunting him, and it scared him to death.

Emma's face softened and her eyes became kinder. She walked around the bed and sat down in front of him. He felt a familiar craving flush through him, a sudden urge to grasp the back of her neck and pull her lips to his. It triggered a wave of nausea and heat in his stomach.

'Lucky,' said Emma, 'listen to me. You are a strong man, but whatever this sickness is, it will finish you if you stay in this room.'

Lucky looked into her emerald eyes. He remembered her arriving at the ranch the day before the funeral, the tightness of her summer clothes as she walked across the yard, the smell of her hair as she embraced him on the steps, the way she had held him a moment too long.

'You don't know what you're talking about, you haven't seen.'

'All I'm trying to tell you is that you can't always trust things,' she said, 'not the way you're seeing them. You're in a bad place right now.'

'You don't understand,' said Lucky.

He closed his eyes and tried not to be sick. When he opened them again, Emma had walked back over to Scott and they were talking in hushed tones. It made him feel nervous. Scott leant down and spoke to the boy and girl. It looked like he was asking them a question. They both looked over at Lucky then nodded their heads, completely at ease in Scott's company. Lucky felt a jealous anger simmering inside him.

'What is it?' he said.

Scott and Emma both walked over and sat on the bed in front of him. 'This is what's going to happen,' said Scott. 'You need to get well again and until you do, they're going to come and stay with us.'

'No, they stay with me.' Lucky tried to stand but his legs buckled beneath him.

'You need help,' said Scott.

'They're not leaving this room,' said Lucky.

'You're sick,' said Emma.

Lucky struggled to find a reply. He buried his head in his arms and dared not look up, because he knew in his heart they were right.

Emma sat down on the floor in front of him. 'We need to get you to a hospital,' she said. 'The kids can stay with us as long as you need and when you're ready, you can get in touch. You need to finish this, Lucky. Get well and find whoever wrote that letter, find yourself some truth.'

Lucky's mouth tasted dry again. He felt heavy and useless. He thought how pitiful it would be to die on a filthy brown carpet, weak and helpless and surrounded by cheap broken glass. He could feel the sickness overpowering him, his face burning up and stomach churning, as the sunlight in the room grew brighter. Emma's face blurred out of focus and the room began to sway. He looked around him. It felt as though he was trapped inside a photographic negative, all black silhouettes and blinding whiteness. The water spots on the ceiling began to move, floating into each other, collapsing and dividing and re-emerging like the blood cells of some enormous unseen beast, and only Emma appeared real now, the rest of the room and its inhabitants melting into nothingness. He followed the curves of her body as she crouched in front of him.

I still want you, he thought to himself.

Emma froze and stared at him. Her eyes narrowed into dark slits. He realised to his dismay that he had spoken aloud.

She leaned in towards him. 'You'll never change. You're an animal.'

Or at least that's what he thought she said, as the tinnitus rang in his ears and a white light enveloped them both.

MICHELLE SCORZIELLO

Invisible

'OF ALL THE PLACES, *Mulligan's.*'

Margaret pulled a chair from the table in the bay window and set it down in front of the sofa where Lavender sat, their knees just avoiding each other's.

'Men in vests and women who dye their hair so blonde it's luminous.' She scrutinised Lavender's face while she dabbed at the tears, which had wended their way through wrinkles and creases before pooling into grubby stains. 'What on earth possessed you?'

Lavender tugged her face free and bowed her head, her hands twisting a damp tissue into tiny scraps on her lap.

Margaret crossed her arms and waited. After collecting Lavender from the police station at ten o'clock in the evening, she felt nothing short of a full explanation could mitigate such an inconvenience. What a sight Lavender was in her limp pin-tuck blouse with its scratched pearl buttons and her old houndstooth skirt. She'd told Lavender to give the skirt to the Samaritans last year. And where was that ludicrous hat she had bought on Monday, the one with the cherries dangling from it? Lavender had worn it all week and Margaret hadn't the heart to tell her it looked, well, odd. She studied her own nice worsted turquoise skirt; how lovely and sharp and fresh it looked. In the mirror above the sofa she could see the clarity of it reflected in her countenance. She was a small, neat woman, with the black-eyed expression of a humble but inquisitive shrew; the only hint of a tendency towards impatience – she berated herself for such a quality – lay in the tightly drawn line of her mouth, which at this moment caused her thin lips almost to disappear.

'He told me to do it.'

Lavender's voice was so small that Margaret dared not miss a word through the noise of her own inspiration. When no further utterance came, she frowned and drank a large draught of air, a bit like a diver does before plunging into the deep.

'Who did, dear?'

'The barman.'

The white nodes of tissue looked grey on the houndstooth skirt, beneath which Margaret could see the outline of Lavender's small knees. Knees which Margaret had never seen, but which had, allegedly, been exposed in all their white, bony nakedness. She brushed her foot sideways on the Axminster to dislodge Lavender from her thoughts and lowered her voice to what she hoped was a gentle searching whisper.

'Why did you do it? Why?'

'Couldn't keep his eyes off me.'

Lavender looked into Margaret's eyes as if to test the effect of her words before returning to the tissue, which she attempted to open.

'But . . . Lavender, he was so young . . .'

'Do you doubt me? Many men like attractive older women.'

Well, you're certainly older, you got *that* right, Margaret thought. 'What did he say?'

'He said he bet I had a lovely body.' Lavender nodded as if to confirm the authenticity of the statement.

It's a bloody psychiatrist she needs, thought Margaret, as her lips arced in a grimace of incredulity.

Margaret had been telephoned just at the end of *Brief Encounter*, where Celia Johnson and Trevor Howard are waiting for his train before they part forever, and a friend of Johnson's happens upon them and proceeds to prattle on and on and all the while the two lovers are screaming internally as their last seconds together ebb away in the woman's wittering. It was Margaret's favourite scene of the film and she especially enjoyed the build-up to this point. She had almost ignored the ringing of the phone, such was her penchant for the nerve-wracking parting. On and on and on blathers the woman while Johnson and Howard writhe in mute emotional agony. She hadn't been quite focused when she took the call.

'Mrs Hamilton? Mrs Margaret Hamilton?' said a man's voice, mature, softly northern and official.

'This is she.'

'P.C. Giddens from Kingston Police. I have Lavender Withers here.'

'Lavender? Did you say Lavender?'

'Could you come and collect her? We have no cars available for at least an hour and she's feeling . . . a little fragile . . .'

*

No doubt about it, a new item of clothing did much for one's expansiveness, thought Lavender, and as she trotted along in the late summer sun, she caught sight of her own hat shadow, the cherries stretching and sighing in time with her step. Her hesitation over the purchase had proved unfounded. The hat was a hit, she could feel it. Her back felt longer and her neck, why her neck was positively regal! Oh, it was too perfect. She felt giddy and alive and invincible. The very street seemed to twinkle and sparkle as if reflecting back her own incandescence. This evening she would be gay and witty and just a trifle rakish; she pictured herself sitting at the bar, her hands clutching . . . her hands clutching . . . now what was that cocktail she used to drink? The bartender would help . . . her hands clutching the drink and her crossed legs swinging whilst *bon mots* fell from her lips.

How could a hat perform such miracles? Here she was, a sixty-nine-year-old retired German teacher, a spinster, who had never set foot inside a public house in . . . it must be thirty years. But the hat had found her, and this hat with its daring, its aplomb, had caused such a racket within her body that she knew, she just knew, she had to DO SOMETHING.

The door of Mulligan's still wore the faded golden-lettered 'Saloon'. She entered to the low whine of piped music and the smell of stale beer. Grimacing, she planted her right foot forward towards a mock-velvet-topped stool fixed before the bar.

She took in the purple strip-lighting, the purple cushions scattered along the wall-mounted sofas and the long, suspended purple light-shades, and she nodded before twisting open the clasp of her stiff black handbag to check for her glasses case.

The bar was almost empty, save for a few regulars strung out around the perimeter. She balanced a hand on the fat round pad of a stool and hoisted herself up. Her hat, being made of wool, suddenly felt warm under the purple lights. Spying a row of pegs near the entrance, she decided it might be lovely to admire the cherries from afar. So she hurried over and, with careful symmetry, balanced the hat on one of the long, narrow hooks. Stepping back, she reached up a thin, white hand and straightened it as one does a framed painting. *Ausgezeichnet*, she muttered. *Excellent.*

Back on the stool, she gazed in awe at the rows of bottles which filled the mirrored wall with a multitude of shapes and colours – the teacher in her rose up and began to categorise them. She enjoyed doing this until the young barman approached. He stood before her, saying nothing, his whole body forming a question.

'Ah,' said Lavender with a smile that showed she came prepared to be affable.

He chewed gum and his shoulders slumped. He turned his head towards the corner table where three young blondes, all thigh and eyeliner, threw their heads together and laughed, arms gripping each other's elbows, cigarettes waving aloft.

Lavender scanned the bottles, head turning from side to side while her fingers untwisted and snapped shut the clasp of her handbag.

'May I have a gin and tonic, please.' She felt this last word a mistake; it seemed to pulsate in the air like a mimicking echo.

The bartender reached for a bottle (no bright label, not off the shelf, she felt disappointed) and poured, chewing, his eyes fixed on the blondes.

Lavender knew indifference. Years ago – she must have been twenty, in her first job out of teacher training college – she had entered a bar with a crowd of colleagues who'd quickly formed into small natural groups, little clusters of *tête-à-têtes*, the men warmly demonstrating their solicitousness towards the women by ordering their drinks from the bar. She found herself stranded on her own, shut out from the laughing circles and, standing in the midst of them all, she had been suddenly and crushingly aware that no one desired her company. Shrinking from the prospect of approaching the bar herself, and the shame of needing to purchase her own drink, she had taken refuge in the ladies' room and emerged much later, slipping through the crowd of people to the doors and the outside street. They hadn't even registered her absence. She had been invisible.

'Thank you, *vielen Dank*.' She gave a little laugh but the bartender had already retreated to the furthest end of the bar, as near as possible to the blondes, where he took up a cloth and began to polish a glass. One of the blondes whispered into her friend's ear and set off a loud squeal of laughter and an indulgent grin reached across the barman's face. Lavender sipped her drink and enjoyed the bitter sweetness as it slithered down through her chest.

She had drunk her first gin and tonic in her teens, at a party where a boy she admired was certain to be in attendance. She'd met him at a dance weeks earlier – Tom. He smiled at her and put his arm around her and she lived heady on the weight of that arm for days. Knowing he would be at the party, she had taken particular care with her dress that evening and put a white rose in her hair and pinched a clandestine sip of her father's sherry.

Lavender's face softened now as she remembered the boy's brown curls and square shoulders. She stirred her gin with the plastic cocktail stirrer; the ice cubes caught the purple light from the bar.

The party had been held at the house of a girl called Grace. A live band played in the garden and Grace sang and all the young men sighed and Lavender's pluck faltered. Later, in the lounge, as the evening dwindled into intimate raucousness, a group of young men clustered around a magazine like ants around sugar, and through a gap in their shoulders Lavender caught a glimpse of the open pages: a woman and a man, the woman's thighs, her naked breasts, the man's – well, it had been a shock. The young men leered over the open page, jockeying and whooping, and the rose in Lavender's hair wobbled in the press of bodies. She reached up to pull it out just as Tom turned mid-shout, 'What a pair . . .' His eyes locked with hers and for a moment there passed an uncomfortable communication: *What about me, Tom, chaste little me?* He looked away but not before she caught the unmistakable look of discomfort in his eyes.

She stared down at her glass, rimed still with mist that chilled her fingertips. The barman remained at the opposite end of the bar; she was as irrelevant as a stray button.

Finishing her drink, she grasped the handle of her bag and looked to her hat. But only a scarf dangled like a withering vine from the pegs. She blinked, scanning the floor, while behind her the blondes set off a fresh burst of screams.

'Excuse me?'

She was off her stool.

'Excuse me?'

She rushed towards the barman. *Why did he not hear her?*

'My hat . . . my hat is missing.' She pointed at the pegs. 'I hung it there ten minutes ago. It's gone.' Her voice was shrill.

The barman dragged his eyes from the blondes and squinted in mild annoyance.

'Wha'?'

'My hat's gone!'

He scratched the back of his head, shook his shoulders, 'Dunno . . .'

A familiar feeling of despair gathered in Lavender's chest and small tears pricked at her eyelids. The blondes screeched again and the barman's eyes swivelled back to them, his face resuming a look of male intoxication. Lavender was just about to harry him further when she noticed the look on his face change; it became compassionate, approving what it feasted on. She caught the momentary flicker of doubt as he glanced uncomfortably in her direction.

She wheeled around.

One of the girls was standing with the hat on her head, her teeth extended in a horrible horsey parody, her eyes closed in mock rapture. The friends rocked with laughter, as now a simpering smile accompanied the girl's slit eyes. As she moved her head, teasing each friend with scrupulous fairness, the hat wobbled and fell into the grey sediment of the ashtray, sending a glass of red wine tumbling. The little cherries, saturated in the downpour, bobbed into the grey detritus, coating themselves in grit. One of the other girls screamed and leaped up, pulling her dress away from the chaos of the table.

'Oh,' gasped Lavender.

The girls turned. The pair who were standing hurried back to their chairs and the three blonde heads huddled and shook as parps of suppressed mirth leaked from their clamped mouths.

Lavender walked to the girls' table and lifted the hat. Wine dripped like blood on to the floor.

'How *dare* you!'

Holding the hat in her outstretched arm, she turned to the barman whose head shifted away from her, even though his eyes remained on the hat. At his undisguised wince and his obvious intention of doing nothing (what could he do?), Lavender's shoulders folded and her head sagged.

The blondes continued to giggle and whisper and the music played on with airy indifference.

Flooded by the sudden potency of the gin, a strange feeling came over Lavender. Her head felt disconnected from her body and a fine buzz filled her ears. She let loose her shoulders, unfurled her hands and allowed her neck to fold soft as a swan's. The hat fell to the floor.

She thought of Tom and the naked girl in the magazine.

She lifted her head, and slid before the barman just as he placed, with determined intention, one polished glass on the bar. She traced his eyes until they were caught, wrenched and anchored in horror as she let the houndstooth skirt drop to the floor . . .

*

Margaret found her in the waiting area, sitting on a bench huddled over her handbag, a man-sized health and safety jacket draped around her shoulders. A policewoman took Margaret aside, explained *sotto voce* how they had been called to the bar, found Lavender and escorted her back to the station.

'We managed to get your name out of her but very little else. Has she done this type of thing before?'

Margaret led her back to their rooms and began the delicate task of discovering from Lavender's own mouth what had occurred earlier that evening.

'But couldn't you just be content with the compliment, dear?'

She watched Lavender scrutinise the woolly clump of soggy tissue with that curious intensity for a workaday object which strangely seizes hold of people in distress; she turned the scrap over and over in her hands. Then Lavender looked up and stared through Margaret's tight little white-bloused middle; a basking smile illuminated her face, which looked rejuvenated, as if lit from within by the most satisfying of memories.

Margaret sighed and picked up the remote control. She sat down next to Lavender just as the whistle blew for Trevor Howard's train.

SARA CABA
Collages

YOUR HUSBAND and your therapist helped you prepare. In two months you would go home to Costa Rica to see your mother for the first time in five years. 'Why don't you talk to her?' Larry asked you during your first therapy session, a year ago. Your husband John was sitting on the opposite end of the long leather sofa you shared, staring in silence at his boots. You looked outside before giving an answer, gazing over Boston, your husband's home town, with its November snow and grey skies. You thought of your mother back in Costa Rica. You imagined her sleeping – it would only be dawn there – her body wrapped in heavy blankets, sweating in her dark and stuffy room, with its permanent sour smell and night tables stacked up with pills for insomnia, depression, anxiety and weight loss. You looked back at Larry, who was waiting for your answer, and you said: 'I've killed her, she doesn't exist to me.'

Larry shook his head, opened his mouth slowly and said, 'No one can do that.'

You glared at him. You didn't want a judgement; you wanted him to ask you about her. 'Tell me more,' Larry said as if able to read your thoughts. You told him her name was Leonora and she liked the booze. You talked about the sound of her high heels approaching the front door late at night, marching across the ceramic tiles of the house, coming close to the room where you pretended to be asleep. You told him about the pounding of your heart and the crystalline silence that preceded the sound of her grainy voice calling out for you and your brother. 'Bang!' You shouted when describing the noise the door made when she slammed it open. You talked about the blinding light of the bulb and the bloated figure of a woman holding a drink in one hand, a cigarette in the other. Your face twitched when you told him about her pointing finger, her long red nails that liked to poke at your flesh, about her favourite belt and the way she rattled it in the air before landing it on both of you. Finally, you told him how she slapped you and called you *slut* when she found out that you'd had sex for the first time. You talked fast, with no pause, your husband sitting at the far end of the sofa, still staring at his boots. Larry's brown eyes became watery and soft and his body leaned towards you. 'I know,' he nodded when you stopped, 'I know exactly who she is.'

That was a year ago. Now your husband was sitting next to you, holding your hands as you told Larry about your trip to Costa Rica. It would be your first visit with John, it would be your first visit since you left five years ago. 'You will need to be there for her,' Larry said to him, 'you will need to be the husband she needs you to be.' John squeezed your hands inside his and brought them to his lips. 'I know,' he said, 'I will be.'

*

Your brother Ricardo had organised the reunion via email. Your brother with whom you barely spoke, your brother who loved family and had created one of his own, with his plump wife and his charming little boy.

'Hello Sis,' he said when he called the day before to confirm the final details. You frowned and stared at the tropical plants growing outside. He had never called you *Sis* before. 'How are you?' he asked.

'Fine,' you said, accepting the role that he was giving you. 'I'm fine,' you repeated. 'It's been a long time.'

'It has Sis, it has,' he said and paused. 'Tomorrow at 2 p.m., barbeque at my mother's house,' he continued.

'She's also my mother,' you said.

'Sorry, of course, tomorrow at 2 p.m. at our mother's house, all the family will be there.'

'Cool,' you said and hung up, wondering who exactly made up that family. You imagined distant cousins, fat and with beards, sipping their drinks, ripping the meat that hung from soggy *tortillas*. You could hear the *bachata* and *salsa* that they would play after a few too many drinks, the drunken chattering of adults, the background laughter of kids playing on the grass. You saw plump wives serving the men and gossiping about kitchen appliances, you saw the tight ass of your brother's wife moving around your mother, filling the vacant space you left behind, and you saw your mother, in the centre of it all, sitting in a tall chair, overlooking the crowd with a solemn expression while sipping rum and coke. You wiped the sweat from your palms on your jeans when you hung up. 'Are you okay?' John asked. 'I don't know,' you answered. A year ago you would have said, 'Yeah, I'm fine, never mind,' but now you let yourself doubt and you let him hold you and caress your hair.

You borrowed a friend's car to get to your mother's house. You drove slowly, hesitating between one gear and the next. The day was hot and humid; your husband, unused to the heat, sweated in the seat by your side. 'I love you, you know?' you said to him as you drove through the city where you were born. 'I know,' he said and rubbed your cheek with his warm hand. You were late, half an hour late. A queue of cars was already parked outside your mother's yellow house; you recognised none of them.

You walked slowly up the path to the front door. The same path that, night after night, your mother walked in high heels. You had sandals on, flat sandals which made no sound. The door was opened. You took a deep breath before stepping in. The crowd in the dining room went quiet. Most faces were remote, as if from another life. There was a new one among them, a tanned two-year-old boy. My nephew, you thought, the word sounding weird in your head. Your eyes flipped through family faces until you reached that of your mother. She was sitting in the centre of it all, but not in a tall chair, just an ordinary one from the dining room set. She seemed shrunken and her eyes were almost shut. You thought about her night tables, full of pills, and wondered how many she had swallowed that same morning and the night before.

A camera flash broke the silence. It was your mother's youngest sister, Anabela, you barely knew her. 'Larita!' she wailed as she trotted towards you. 'Welcome back!' 'Welcome back!' the crowd chanted after her. 'And this must be the husband!' she said, after releasing you from a tight hug. 'Oh! But look how handsome he is!' she said and turned John's body so the crowd could see the white American man that you had brought home. You walked along with your husband delivering kisses to people you hadn't seen since you were a child. Family, as your brother had said. You tousled the hair of the little brown boy who was your nephew, but he withdrew. He was too young to know that you belonged to the same family. You halted before reaching your mother's chair. People fell silent, more photos were taken. You leaned down to kiss your mother's cheek. It was a quick kiss; a sour vapour was coming out of her mouth. 'It's good to see you, Mom,' you said, and straightened. 'Good to see you too,' she said after you. Her mouth opened wide and she seemed to want to say more, but then she looked exhausted and just smiled. 'This is John,' you said, bringing him in. 'How handsome,' she said as she stared at the whiteness of his skin and the blueness of his eyes. 'Come sit next to me, John,' she ordered him; John complied and smiled. He sat by her side and began patiently to answer her interrogation about salary, education and family plans. You sat at a distance, answering random questions that came in your direction, watching your husband and your mother talk.

*

Despite your brother's efforts to keep the family around, everyone left early. Minutes later he followed them, and in a matter of seconds it was just you, your mother, and John.

'Well,' your mother said, staring at a dozen empty chairs, 'so good to have you both home.' Her eyes were glossy, tiny. 'Do you fancy a drink?' she said reaching for the minibar next to her. 'It's hot in here,' she said as she poured some ice, three quarters of rum and a pinch of diet coke into a tall glass.

'I'm fine,' John said. 'Thank you very much.'

You didn't say anything. You stared at your mother's bent head, at the liquid slipping quickly down her throat.

'John,' she said when she had finished half of the glass, 'it is so nice to finally meet you. I would have liked to go to the wedding, but well, it wasn't possible. Anyways, let's not talk about sad things.'

'We'll have to get married here in Costa Rica too,' John smiled at her, 'and you will be the guest of honour.'

'Oh, that would be nice John, that would be so nice.' She took a long gulp and finished her drink.

Your shoulders were tense. You wanted to stretch your arm and ditch the empty glass from her veined hand. You stared at her long red nails, chipped at the front. You hated those red nails.

'Larita, honey,' she said as if reading your thoughts, 'why don't you go to my room and get a photo album to show some pictures to John. They are under my bed.'

'Sure, Mom,' you said and left the seat right away.

The salon that used to feel enormous as a child felt tiny now. You stopped in the centre of the room and observed the three doors that opened into it. You walked towards your brother's first and opened it slowly. His surfing posters and the bust of Lenin on the night table that used to belong to your father were gone, replaced by an impersonal desk, some bookshelves and an old computer. You closed the door and walked half a metre towards the room where you had lived until you were nineteen, when you left on a six-month student exchange to the States and never came back. You held the doorknob in your damp hand and hesitated before turning it. You wanted to remember how that room looked the last time you were there. You had a white rattan bed with matching dressing table, embroidered, fit for a princess; you had Barbies on the shelves, even though you hadn't played with them since you were twelve; you had photos of your friends from high school on the walls; and in a drawer of your night table a photo of your first boyfriend, sprayed with his cologne. Slowly, you turned the knob and looked in at a narrow bed sitting alone in the middle of the room. Your bed, that bed where you made love for the first time, was gone. You wanted to cry but you didn't. You turned and rushed across the living room. The door to your mother's room was open. It was dark and stuffy in there, as it had always been. The bed was undone, the sheets looked gritty under the pale light, and high-heeled shoes were scattered all over the carpeted floor. You looked at the walls, bare except for that large frame where your mother used to have a picture of herself with your dad on their wedding day. The photo had been replaced with a sepia picture of your mom as a child, a chubby little girl with a large bow on her head and orthopaedic white shoes. You stared at the photo and wondered how that girl had ever became the woman sitting outside.

Underneath the bed you found a mountain of loose photos and albums. Some of the loose ones had holes replacing heads; some had been crumpled to death. You picked the album closest to your hand – it was dusty and mouldy down there – and you returned to the dining room, where your mother was holding a second drink.

'Here,' you said clenching your teeth.

'Thank you, Larita.'

Larita? Sis? you mused as you sat down. What are they trying to prove?

'Okay, so let's see what we have here,' your mother said and wetted her index finger in her mouth before opening the dusty burgundy album and staring at old black-and-white photos. She remained silent, puzzled. Perhaps they were photos of some family she didn't even recognise. She flipped quickly through those pages until she reached a familiar face.

'Look Larita! I didn't know I still had a photo of him!'

'Who is it?' John asked.

'It's Marco,' you said, 'he was – '

'He was Larita's first boyfriend. Oh, such a handsome and respectful young man, and he came from such a good family.'

Your body trembled. She sure didn't think that the day she slapped you in the face and called you *slut* and locked you in your room for two days.

'Oh, no offence, please!' she said to John, placing her hand on his shoulder. 'Nothing compared to you!'

John smiled and patted her hand.

'Have you heard from him, Larita?'

'No, Mother, I haven't. I haven't been his girlfriend for more than seven years. I have been living abroad for five . . .'

'Oh, sure, how silly of me. Say hi from me if you ever see him or talk to him.'

'Mother . . .' you said, pointing at John with your eyes.

'Oops!' she blurted and covered her mouth. 'It's so hot, isn't it? So hot!' she said, pulling her high heels off her feet. Her toes, deformed by years of torture, dangled in the air. 'John, would you mind?' she said passing her empty glass to him.

You glared at her.

'He's family now,' she said.

'It's okay,' John said, 'I don't mind. Here.'

'Thank you, angel. You really look like an angel, did you know that?'

'Mom . . . the photos.'

'Yes, yes, the photos. Let's see,' she said wiping the sweat from her forehead.

'Oh, no, not these, these are so blurry!' she said as she moved quickly through a set of beach photos where she looked drunk or hungover, or both. 'Awful!'

You stared at her long red nails, skipping the dog-eared pages of the album, and felt sick. Those beach holidays, that *salsa* and *bachata* playing until dawn, the sprinkled toilets, the rancid bedding; it all came flooding back to your present.

'Are you okay, Lara?' John asked.

It was good to hear your name, Lara, it was good to hear it from him.

'A little hot,' you said, 'I'll be fine, thanks for asking.'

'Oh! Look what I found here!' your mother shouted while placing her almost empty glass on the table in front of her.

'Do you remember, Larita?' she asked with a melodramatic voice as she showed you the picture of your ninth birthday celebration.

'Not really, no.'

Your mother shrunk a little in her chair and her brown eyes looked grey for a moment.

'Oh, well,' she said scratching her chin with a long red nail. 'It was a gorgeous day. Sunny, breezy. I left work early, went to the salon to have a perm done. You know, it was the 80s,' she turned towards John, 'and when I was there I got tempted into dying it blonde. I wanted to look good for my little girl's eighth birthday. I got her this cake, an ice-cream cake, you know she loves ice-cream cakes, don't you John? So I had booked this appointment in this great pastry shop, very exclusive, and had them make a cake especially for Larita. I picked it up, with my blonde perm freshly done, and drove home, where I had a present for Larita, one of those Barbies she played with until she was nineteen, until she went away. Well, we all had a great time, Ricardo, Larita, and me. Her father was travelling those days. We sang the birthday song, and we blew out the candles and then we used this fancy camera to take this photo for us. Look at it, John! Isn't it gorgeous?'

'It is, Mrs Leonora, it really is,' John said, as he caressed your tense hand and brought it to his lips.

'Larita,' your mother said in a lower voice after finishing her drink, 'you really can't remember any of it? Not a tiny bit?'

You stared at her, at her bloated figure occupying a tiny wooden chair, and shook your head. Of course you remembered, you remembered well. Your father wasn't travelling; your father had left the house two months before, never to return, and it wasn't a breezy and sunny day but an oppressively humid one. You were turning nine, not eight, the day that your mother entered through the door, zig-zagging in her high heels, with a shopping bag in one hand, wearing a new shiny yellow dress, styling a horrible blonde perm. She turned pale when she saw you sitting in your school uniform, watching the late afternoon cartoons. She halted and tiptoed out of the house, back into the streets, and appeared an hour later, with a melting ice-cream cake, even though you were allergic to dairy, and a Barbie you already had. She placed one of those long white candles you used when there was no electricity in the house in the middle of the cake and called out for your brother, who was locked in his room, and after singing, quickly, so the cake wouldn't disappear, she pinched both of you in the arm so you would smile, because the automatic camera, which your father should have been there to operate, was about to take a photo, a photo that would make it into the family albums and would become a fundamental part of the memory of a family you never were and would never be.

'Well,' your mother said, breaking the silence, staring down at her damaged feet. 'It's late. Perhaps you're tired, perhaps you want to go.'

You looked at her and knew that she would be sitting in that same chair in the same position for hours after your departure, drinking more rum and cola, alone, counting the empty chairs as she caressed the dusty album crying silently until an unbearable exhaustion made her leave the seat and drag her feet towards her dark room, where she would slide into her clammy bed, swallow a combination of pills and stare for endless hours at the child with rosy cheeks and large bow.

Your eyes were watery and soft when you reached for her. 'No, Mama,' you said, patting the hand that had just closed the photo album. 'Carry on,' you added. You watched as she opened the album with a smile as wide as she could, and continued to build your collages of memories as the afternoon sun set and the end of the day drew near.

Biographies

ELIZABETH BUCK is a Londoner with four adult children who at last are old enough to fend for themselves. She now has time to turn writing for pleasure into something more serious; thanks to the CCWC and family and friends she is now out of the writing 'closet' and embarking on her first novel *Landing the Eagle*. 'Up She Stands' is an extract from this work.

SARA CABA was born and bred in Costa Rica, but for the last eleven years has lived in different countries and with different languages. She is now settled in London and has adopted English as her writing language. She has had short stories published in Spanish and in English. She teaches Spanish as a foreign language to adults, at her own school.

AMANDA COWLEY studied Art and Dance at Roehampton Institute. She was Art Director at Mentorn Films and later pursued landscape painting, holding several exhibitions. *The Granddaughter Clock* is her first novel and is based on the lives of her grandparents. She lives in West London, is married to an Anglican minister, and has a teenage daughter and an adult stepson.

RENUKA DAVID, when she is not working as bean counter, writes novels and screenplays and goes on safari. She also dabbles in writing poetry. Her first novel is buried in a lead box, which is the best place for it, and her next one is on the much-travelled road of being rewritten.

CHARLOTTE EDWARDES is an award-winning journalist and writer. She was a staff writer for *The Sunday Telegraph* and *The Daily Telegraph* for over a decade, covering a broad brief from investigations to the war in Iraq. She currently writes interviews for the *Evening Standard*, and has contributed, among others, to *The Times*, the *Spectator*, *Vogue* and *Tatler*. She has an MA in Middle East history and has travelled extensively in the region. 'Aden' is an extract from her first novel.

ALEX FLATT was born in Norfolk and grew up in the countryside dreaming of urban sprawl and diesel-stained city living. For the last thirteen years Alex has lived and worked in London on both the eeast and west of the subterranean Fleet River.

KEVIN FRANKE is a writer who lives in London. He will never learn that he cannot possibly read books at the speed at which he acquires them. Follow him on Twitter @KevinFrankeUK.

CHARLOTTE GÄBLER-GOES was born in Hamburg. She discovered her love of writing in primary school when she decided that she would become either a writer or an astronaut. She has been writing in English for four years. 'When He Met Death' is an excerpt from her work in progress, a dystopian fantasy for young adults.

LAURENCE JONES was born, raised and lives in London. He works in the City and is currently finishing his first novel, *New Country*, from which 'Two Against One' is an extract.

ARIKE OKE is an archivist and former rollergirl who writes about rivers and cities, memory and loss. She has had stories exhibited ('Artlink', Hull), published (*Words With Jam*, *The Rumpus*) and performed ('Liars League', London, 'Play!', Windsor). She is working on her first novel with the Royal Holloway MA in Creative Writing. She writes a scratch story a month on 'arikewrites'.

MADELINE PARSONS has been writing seriously for about four years. She is particularly interested in the short story form, and has accumulated a small collection of stories. Her writing experience also includes academic essays and a thesis on James Joyce. One of her stories has appeared in a *Words With Jam* anthology.

CELIA REYNOLDS recently embarked on a new career in writing after working for many years in film marketing. As well as writing short stories, she is currently working towards completion of her first novel. Originally from Wales, she now lives in North London.

JOANNA ROSENTHALL is a psychoanalyst and a couple psychotherapist working in the NHS and privately. She is also a writer, has won two short story competitions and has published a number of short stories. She is currently working on a novel. She lives in North London.

BELINDA SADDINGTON was born in Zambia and grew up in southern Africa where she trained as a journalist. She later worked as an advertising copywriter in Zimbabwe before moving to Europe where she qualified as a lawyer. Belinda has published articles in several legal journals and is now working on a murder mystery novel which has its roots in Africa.

AMANDA SAINT works as a freelance writer and 'As if I Were a River' is her first novel. Her short stories have been long-listed in the Fish Flash Fiction Prize and published in *Stories for Homes*. Amanda also runs Retreat West, providing writing retreats, workshops and short story competitions. She lives by the sea on Exmoor with her husband and cat.

MICHELLE SCORZIELLO studied history at University College London. She teaches literacy and numeracy to dyslexic children and writes short stories in her spare time. She is currently writing her memoir about childhood holidays spent in Belfast during the 1970s. Her writing hero is George Orwell.

SHIKO tells the unique stories of those whose paths she has crossed. Her novels are her outlet for experiences in journalism, teaching, business and human rights across the globe. Her travels across six continents give her a challenging range of backdrops and characters. She has been published, won several awards, and written for literary journals since her journey began.

BERNARD SWEET lives in south-west London with his wife and family. After a career in business he now enjoys writing. He has a life-long interest in philosophy and theology but refuses to take either too seriously. He has a degree in philosophy and an MA in Psychology of Religion.

JORDAN TAYLOR is a 21-year-old writer from the United States. He attends Brown University and intends to live in New York City – and keep writing – after graduating.

THOMAS WATSON lives in London. His story 'The Café at the V&A' was awarded second prize in the Seán Ó Faoláin Short Story Competition and is awaiting publication in an anthology. He is working on his first novel.

ANGELA YOUNG's first novel, *Speaking of Love*, was shortlisted for Spread the Word 2008. Her second, *The Dance of Love* (dissenting Edwardian debutante strives to marry for love) has just been submitted to publishers. Her third, *For the Love of Life* (twentieth-century angel of death falls in love with human), is just begun. She holds an MA in Creative Writing. www.angela-young.co.uk

Editor Biographies

MAGGIE HAMAND is a journalist, non-fiction author and novelist. She was winner of the first World One-Day Novel Cup and her winning novel, *The Resurrection of the Body*, was first published by Michael Joseph and has recently been optioned for film. Her second novel, *The Rocket Man*, has also been published, along with several short stories, some of which have been shortlisted for prizes. She taught novel-writing at Morley College, was Writer in Residence at Holloway Prison, and a Royal Literary Fund Fellow at London University of the Arts. She co-founded and directed the award-winning small independent publisher The Maia Press from 2002 to 2010 and has recently published the definitive guide for beginner writers, *Creative Writing For Dummies*.

NATASHA HODGSON has three years of experience in publishing. She is currently editorial assistant at Canongate Books and has previously worked at the literary scout Anne-Louise Fisher Associates and Dorling Kindersley, as well as completing many an internship. She studied French and Italian at Pembroke College, University of Oxford. She is British and Bulgarian, grew up in Indonesia and now lives in London.

EMMANUELLE CHAZARIN was born in France and grew up in Tanzania and Costa Rica. She studied journalism at the University of Sheffield and has worked on the editorial desks of several magazines. She lives in London, enjoys kickboxing, and works as an online content editor for a large travel website.

NATALIE BUTLIN has an MA in creative writing from the University of East Anglia. Having interned at publishing houses and literary agencies, she taught and worked as an editorial assistant for the CCWC. She now works for Christine Green Authors' Agent, a small and highly editorial literary agency, which specialises in fiction.

The Complete
Creative Writing Course

Top-quality creative writing courses at the Groucho
Club in Soho, London's well-known literary venue,
and at the New Cavendish Club, Marble Arch.

The Complete Creative Writing Course has a range
of courses throughout the year to suit your individual
needs, from beginners and intermediate to advanced
courses in fiction writing and also screenwriting
courses and courses in writing for children. We also
run regular weekend workshops and an intensive
summer workshop.

Classes are held on weekday afternoons,
evenings and weekends, and all our tutors
are experienced writers and teachers.
Published former students include Dreda Say Mitchell,
Clare Sambrook and Naomi Wood.

www.writingcourses.org.uk